A LUCKY LUKE ADVENTURE

THE CURSED RANCH

ARTWORK: MORRIS *(WITH THE PARTICIPATION OF M. JANVIER)*
SCRIPT: C. GUYLOUIS *(THE CURSED RANCH – THE STATUE)*
X. FAUCHE AND J. LÉTURGIE *(THE FORTUNE-TELLER)*
J. LÉTURGIE *(THE LOG FLUME)*

Colours: Studio LEONARDO

9th CINEBOOK
The 9th Art Publisher

Original title: Le Ranch Maudit
Original edition: © Dargaud Editeur Paris 1986 by Morris, Guylouis, Fauche & Léturgie
© Lucky Comics
www.lucky-luke.com
English translation: © 2016 Cinebook Ltd
Translator: Jerome Saincantin
Editor: Erica Olson Jeffrey
Lettering and text layout: Design Amorandi
Printed in Spain by EGEDSA
This edition first published in Great Britain in 2016 by
Cinebook Ltd
56 Beech Avenue
Canterbury, Kent
CT4 7TA
www.cinebook.com
A CIP catalogue record for this book
is available from the British Library
ISBN 978-1-84918-320-8

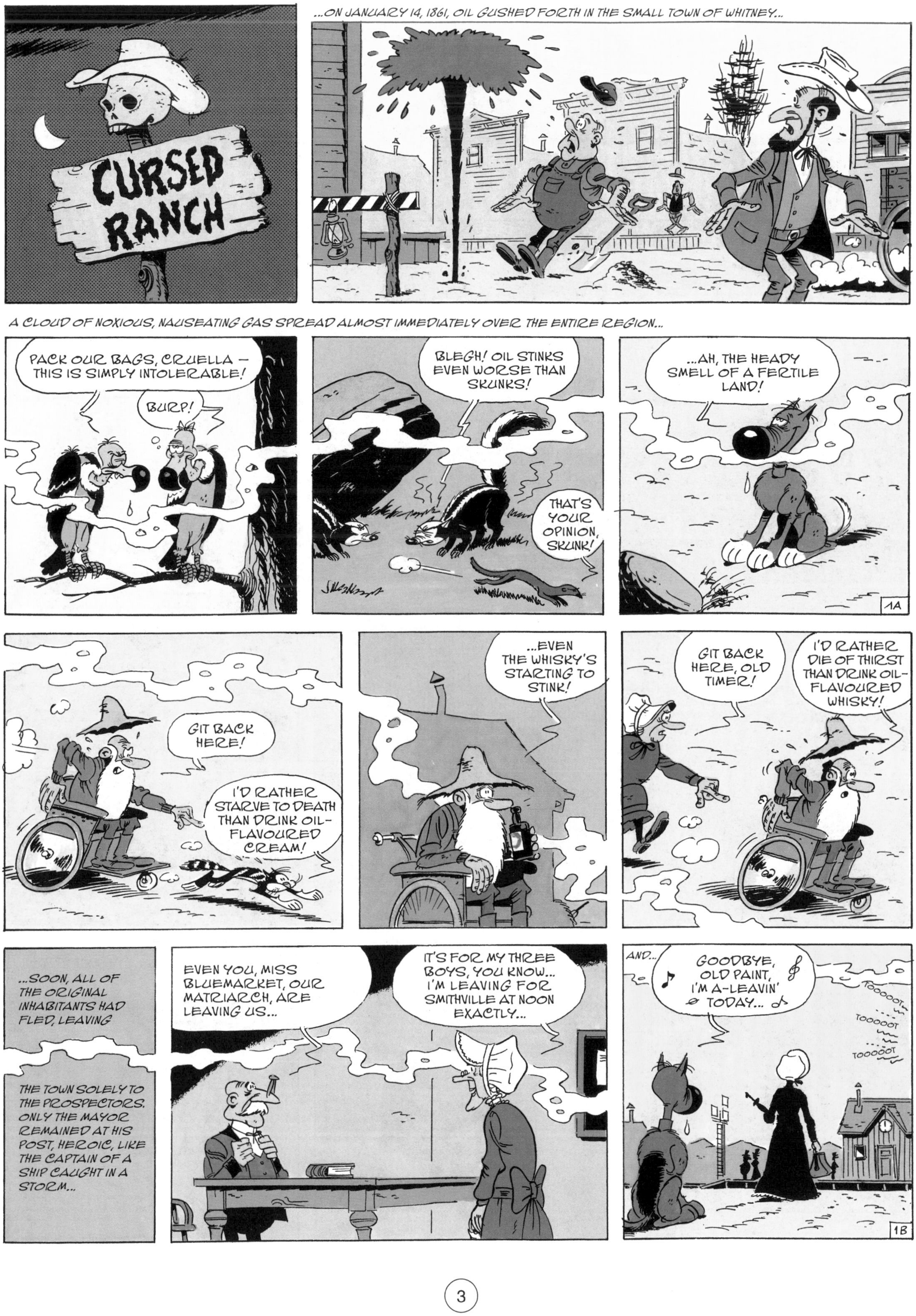
CURSED RANCH
...ON JANUARY 14, 1861, OIL GUSHED FORTH IN THE SMALL TOWN OF WHITNEY...
A CLOUD OF NOXIOUS, NAUSEATING GAS SPREAD ALMOST IMMEDIATELY OVER THE ENTIRE REGION...
PACK OUR BAGS, CRUELLA – THIS IS SIMPLY INTOLERABLE!
BURP!
BLEGH! OIL STINKS EVEN WORSE THAN SKUNKS!
THAT'S YOUR OPINION, SKUNK!
...AH, THE HEADY SMELL OF A FERTILE LAND!
1A
GIT BACK HERE!
I'D RATHER STARVE TO DEATH THAN DRINK OIL-FLAVOURED CREAM!
...EVEN THE WHISKY'S STARTING TO STINK!
GIT BACK HERE, OLD TIMER!
I'D RATHER DIE OF THIRST THAN DRINK OIL-FLAVOURED WHISKY!
...SOON, ALL OF THE ORIGINAL INHABITANTS HAD FLED, LEAVING
THE TOWN SOLELY TO THE PROSPECTORS. ONLY THE MAYOR REMAINED AT HIS POST, HEROIC, LIKE THE CAPTAIN OF A SHIP CAUGHT IN A STORM...
EVEN YOU, MISS BLUEMARKET, OUR MATRIARCH, ARE LEAVING US...
IT'S FOR MY THREE BOYS, YOU KNOW... I'M LEAVING FOR SMITHVILLE AT NOON EXACTLY...
AND...
GOODBYE, OLD PAINT, I'M A-LEAVIN' TODAY...
TOOOOOT
TOOOOOT
TOOOOOT
1B

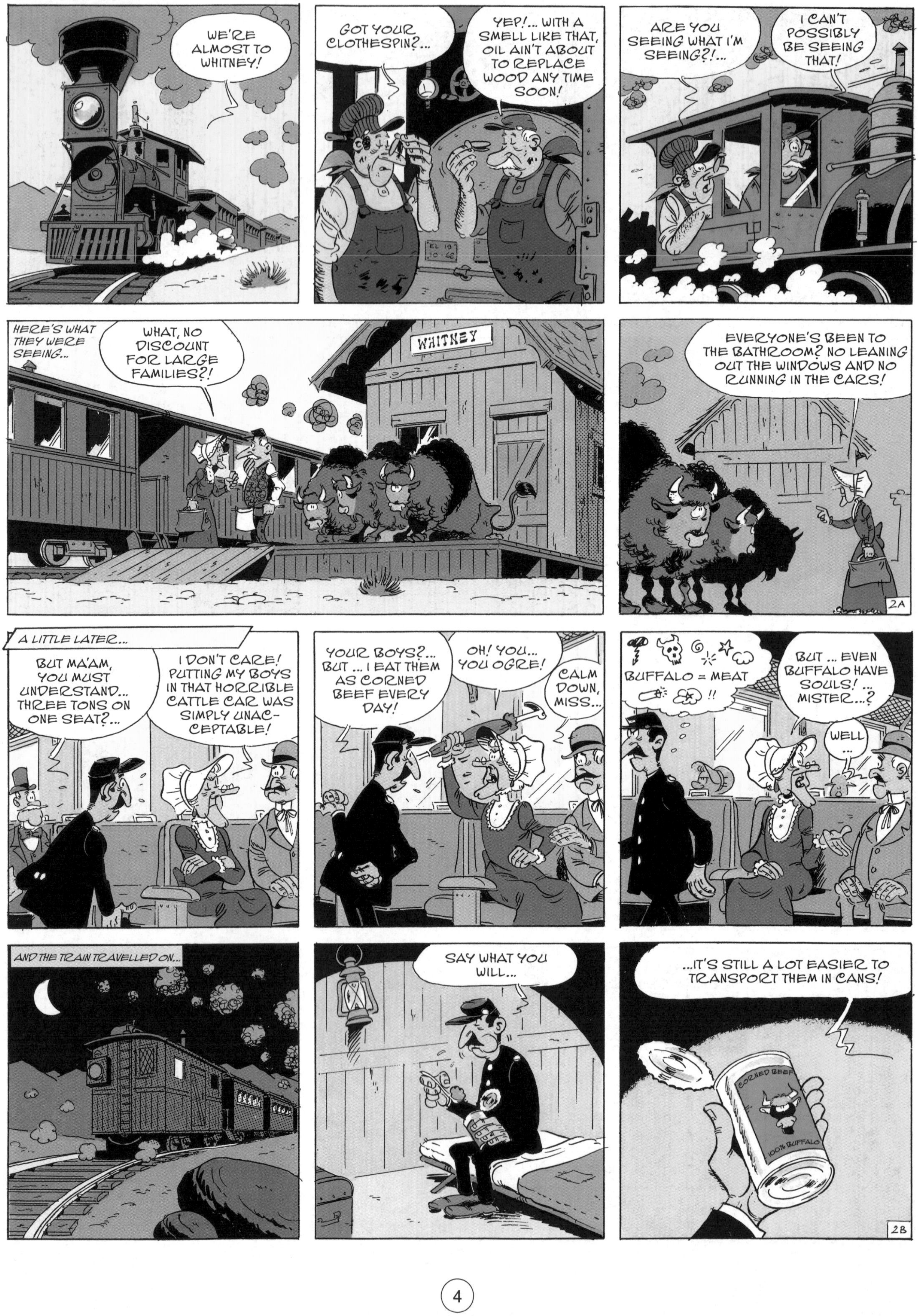
WE'RE ALMOST TO WHITNEY!
GOT YOUR CLOTHESPIN?...
YEP!... WITH A SMELL LIKE THAT, OIL AIN'T ABOUT TO REPLACE WOOD ANY TIME SOON!
ARE YOU SEEING WHAT I'M SEEING?!...
I CAN'T POSSIBLY BE SEEING THAT!
HERE'S WHAT THEY WERE SEEING...
WHITNEY
WHAT, NO DISCOUNT FOR LARGE FAMILIES?!
EVERYONE'S BEEN TO THE BATHROOM? NO LEANING OUT THE WINDOWS AND NO RUNNING IN THE CARS!
2A
A LITTLE LATER...
BUT MA'AM, YOU MUST UNDERSTAND... THREE TONS ON ONE SEAT?...
I DON'T CARE! PUTTING MY BOYS IN THAT HORRIBLE CATTLE CAR WAS SIMPLY UNACCEPTABLE!
YOUR BOYS?... BUT ... I EAT THEM AS CORNED BEEF EVERY DAY!
OH! YOU... YOU OGRE!
CALM DOWN, MISS...
BUFFALO = MEAT
!!
BUT ... EVEN BUFFALO HAVE SOULS! ... MISTER...?
WELL ...
AND THE TRAIN TRAVELLED ON...
SAY WHAT YOU WILL...
...IT'S STILL A LOT EASIER TO TRANSPORT THEM IN CANS!
CORNED BEEF
100% BUFFALO
2B

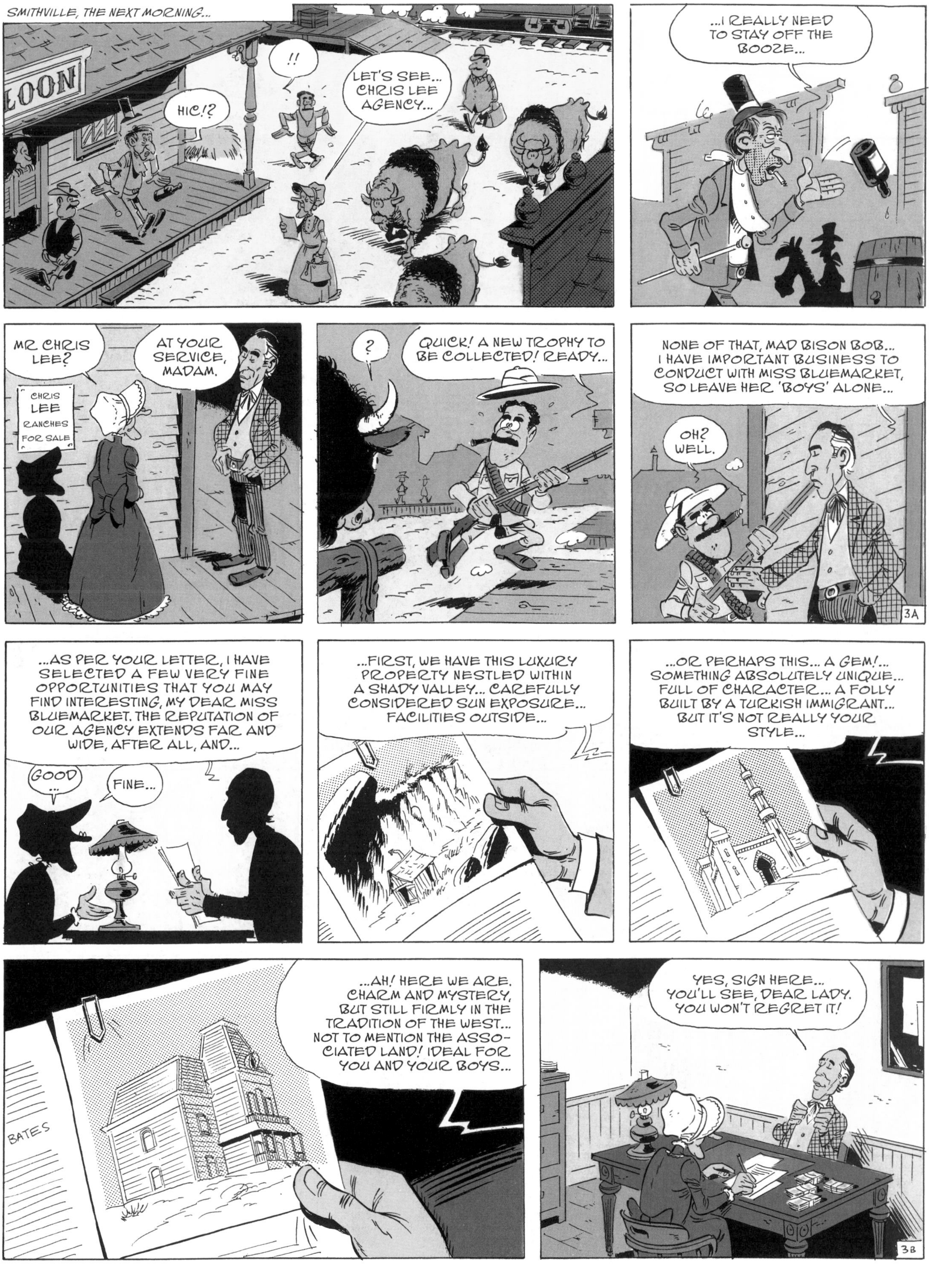

SMITHVILLE, THE NEXT MORNING...
LOON
HIC!?
!!
LET'S SEE... CHRIS LEE AGENCY...
...I REALLY NEED TO STAY OFF THE BOOZE...
MR CHRIS LEE?
AT YOUR SERVICE, MADAM.
CHRIS LEE RANCHES FOR SALE
?
QUICK! A NEW TROPHY TO BE COLLECTED! READY...
NONE OF THAT, MAD BISON BOB... I HAVE IMPORTANT BUSINESS TO CONDUCT WITH MISS BLUEMARKET, SO LEAVE HER 'BOYS' ALONE...
OH? WELL.
3A
...AS PER YOUR LETTER, I HAVE SELECTED A FEW VERY FINE OPPORTUNITIES THAT YOU MAY FIND INTERESTING, MY DEAR MISS BLUEMARKET. THE REPUTATION OF OUR AGENCY EXTENDS FAR AND WIDE, AFTER ALL, AND...
GOOD...
FINE...
...FIRST, WE HAVE THIS LUXURY PROPERTY NESTLED WITHIN A SHADY VALLEY... CAREFULLY CONSIDERED SUN EXPOSURE... FACILITIES OUTSIDE...
...OR PERHAPS THIS... A GEM!... SOMETHING ABSOLUTELY UNIQUE... FULL OF CHARACTER... A FOLLY BUILT BY A TURKISH IMMIGRANT... BUT IT'S NOT REALLY YOUR STYLE...
...AH! HERE WE ARE. CHARM AND MYSTERY, BUT STILL FIRMLY IN THE TRADITION OF THE WEST... NOT TO MENTION THE ASSOCIATED LAND! IDEAL FOR YOU AND YOUR BOYS...
BATES
YES, SIGN HERE... YOU'LL SEE, DEAR LADY. YOU WON'T REGRET IT!
3B

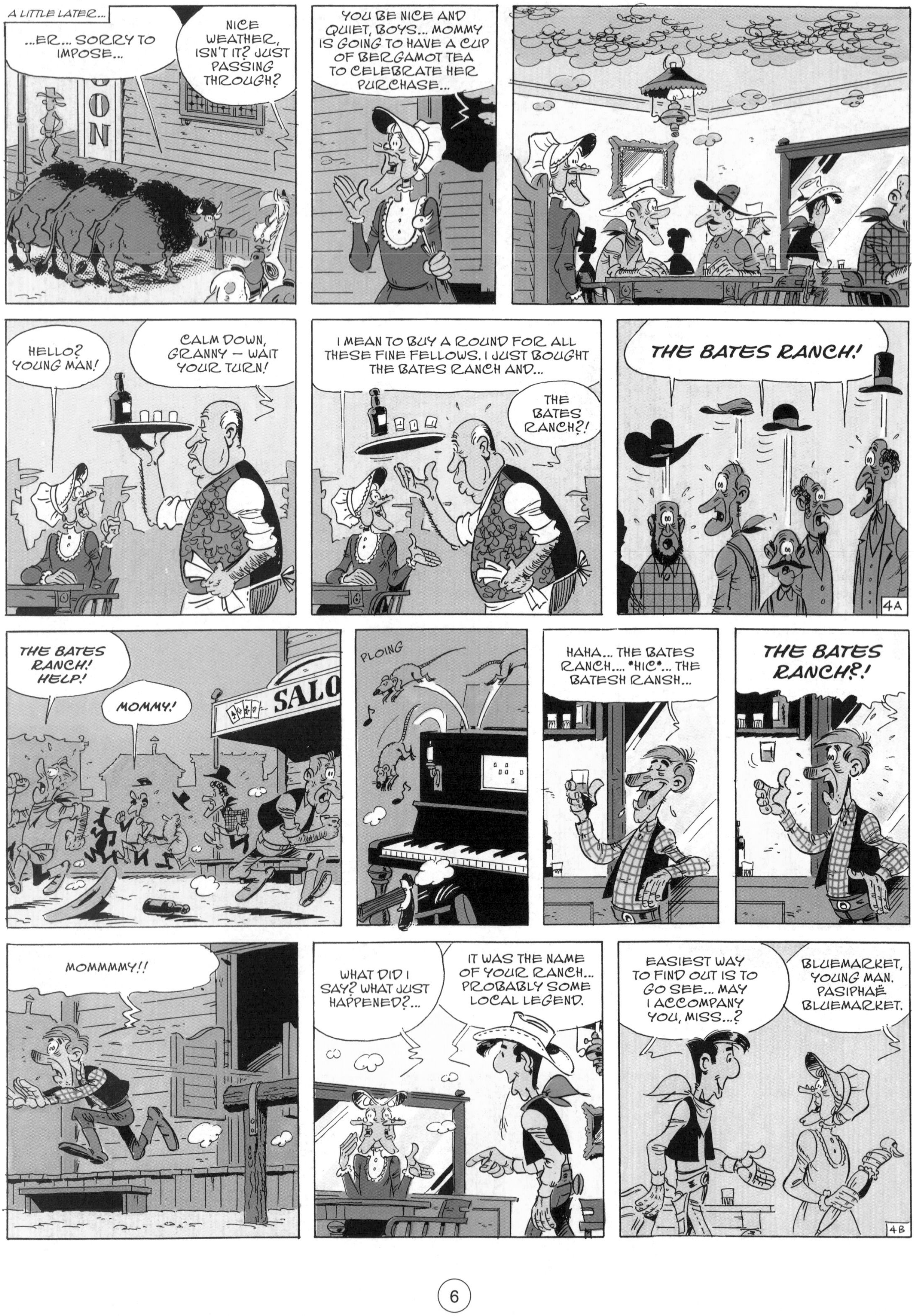
A LITTLE LATER...
...ER... SORRY TO IMPOSE...
NICE WEATHER, ISN'T IT? JUST PASSING THROUGH?
YOU BE NICE AND QUIET, BOYS... MOMMY IS GOING TO HAVE A CUP OF BERGAMOT TEA TO CELEBRATE HER PURCHASE...
HELLO? YOUNG MAN!
CALM DOWN, GRANNY — WAIT YOUR TURN!
I MEAN TO BUY A ROUND FOR ALL THESE FINE FELLOWS. I JUST BOUGHT THE BATES RANCH AND...
THE BATES RANCH?!
THE BATES RANCH!
4A
THE BATES RANCH! HELP!
MOMMY!
SALO
PLOING
HAHA... THE BATES RANCH.... *HIC*... THE BATESH RANSH...
THE BATES RANCH?!
MOMMMMY!!
WHAT DID I SAY? WHAT JUST HAPPENED?...
IT WAS THE NAME OF YOUR RANCH... PROBABLY SOME LOCAL LEGEND.
EASIEST WAY TO FIND OUT IS TO GO SEE... MAY I ACCOMPANY YOU, MISS...?
BLUEMARKET, YOUNG MAN. PASIPHAË BLUEMARKET.
4B

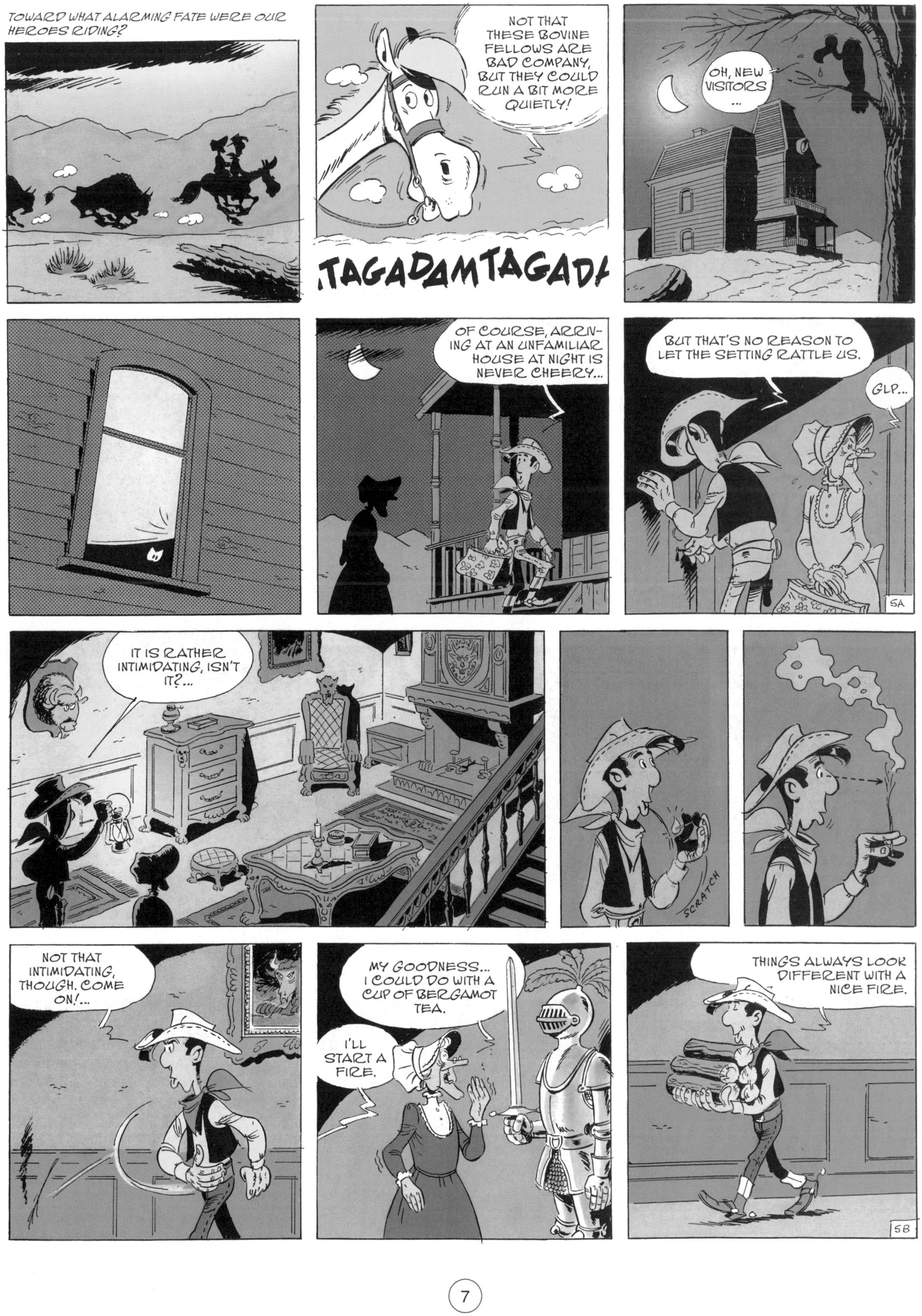
TOWARD WHAT ALARMING FATE WERE OUR HEROES RIDING?
NOT THAT THESE BOVINE FELLOWS ARE BAD COMPANY, BUT THEY COULD RUN A BIT MORE QUIETLY!
TAGADAMTAGADA
OH, NEW VISITORS ...
OF COURSE, ARRIVING AT AN UNFAMILIAR HOUSE AT NIGHT IS NEVER CHEERY...
BUT THAT'S NO REASON TO LET THE SETTING RATTLE US.
GLP...
5A
IT IS RATHER INTIMIDATING, ISN'T IT?...
SCRATCH
NOT THAT INTIMIDATING, THOUGH. COME ON!...
MY GOODNESS... I COULD DO WITH A CUP OF BERGAMOT TEA.
I'LL START A FIRE.
THINGS ALWAYS LOOK DIFFERENT WITH A NICE FIRE.
5B

AAAAAHH...

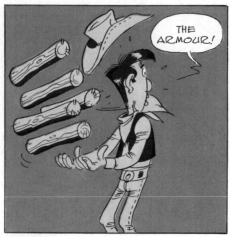

THE ARMOUR!

TSHAK!

TSHAK!

TOK

BANG!

...THAT SURELY WAS BIZARRE!

A GUNSHOT ALREADY?! THIS'LL BE A BUSY NIGHT.

?

CLANG!

WITHIN A FEW MINUTES, STRANGE SILHOUETTES SURROUNDED OUR HERBIVORES...

!

?

MOMMY!

WORRISOME, YES. DANGEROUS, MAYBE. FISHY, DEFINITELY!

THIS PLACE IS STARTING TO GET ON MY NERVES...

COME SEE THIS, COWBOY. WE'VE GOT GUESTS!

?

IT'S MIGHTY LATE TO PAY A VISIT!

MAYBE THEY'VE BROUGHT COOKIES?

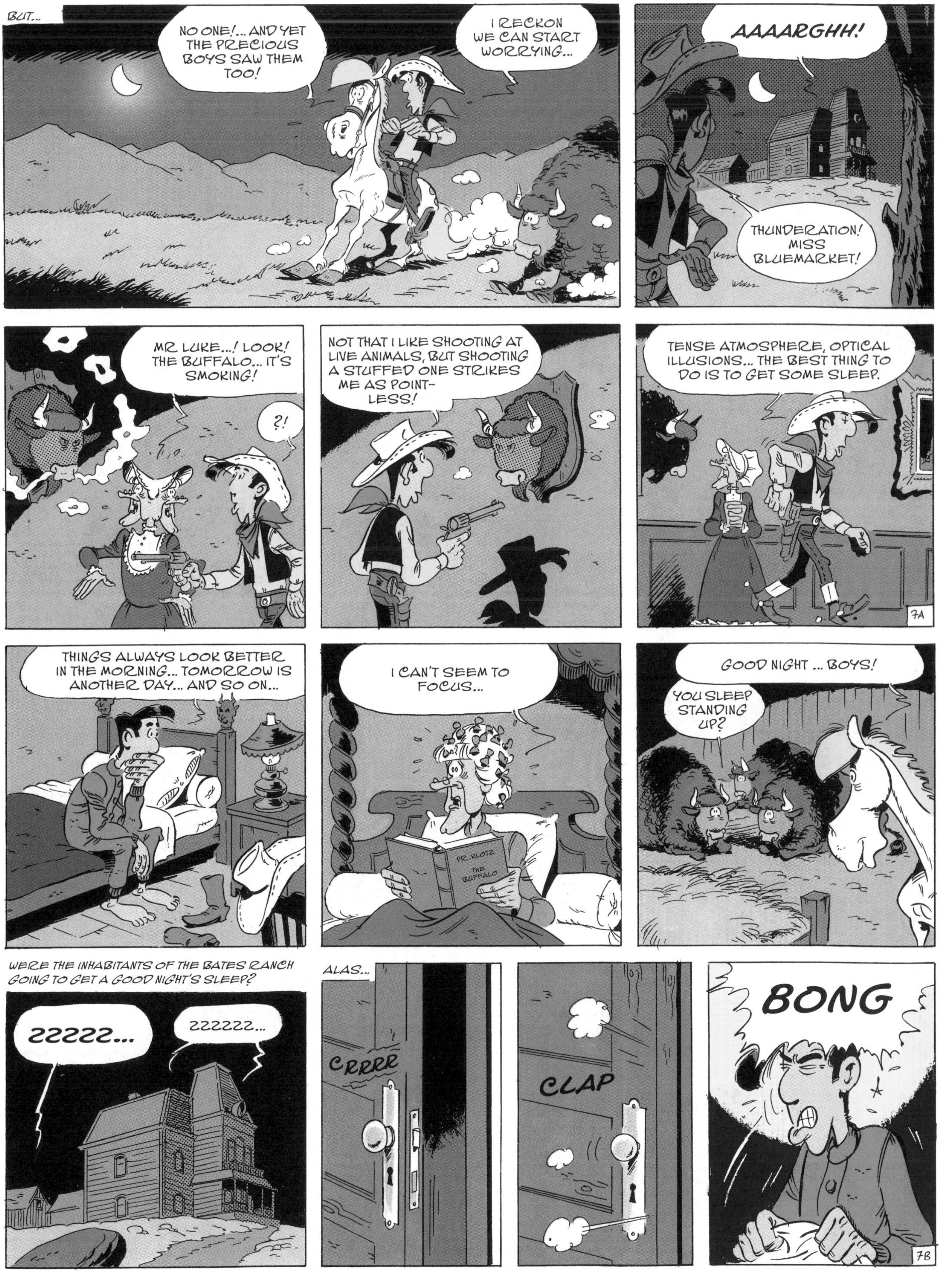
BUT...
NO ONE!... AND YET THE PRECIOUS BOYS SAW THEM TOO!
I RECKON WE CAN START WORRYING...
AAAARGHH!
THUNDERATION! MISS BLUEMARKET!
MR LUKE...! LOOK! THE BUFFALO... IT'S SMOKING!
?!
NOT THAT I LIKE SHOOTING AT LIVE ANIMALS, BUT SHOOTING A STUFFED ONE STRIKES ME AS POINTLESS!
TENSE ATMOSPHERE, OPTICAL ILLUSIONS... THE BEST THING TO DO IS TO GET SOME SLEEP.
7A
THINGS ALWAYS LOOK BETTER IN THE MORNING... TOMORROW IS ANOTHER DAY... AND SO ON...
I CAN'T SEEM TO FOCUS...
PR. KLOTZ
THE BUFFALO
GOOD NIGHT ... BOYS!
YOU SLEEP STANDING UP?
WERE THE INHABITANTS OF THE BATES RANCH GOING TO GET A GOOD NIGHT'S SLEEP?
ZZZZZ...
ZZZZZZ...
ALAS...
CRRRR
CLAP
BONG
7B

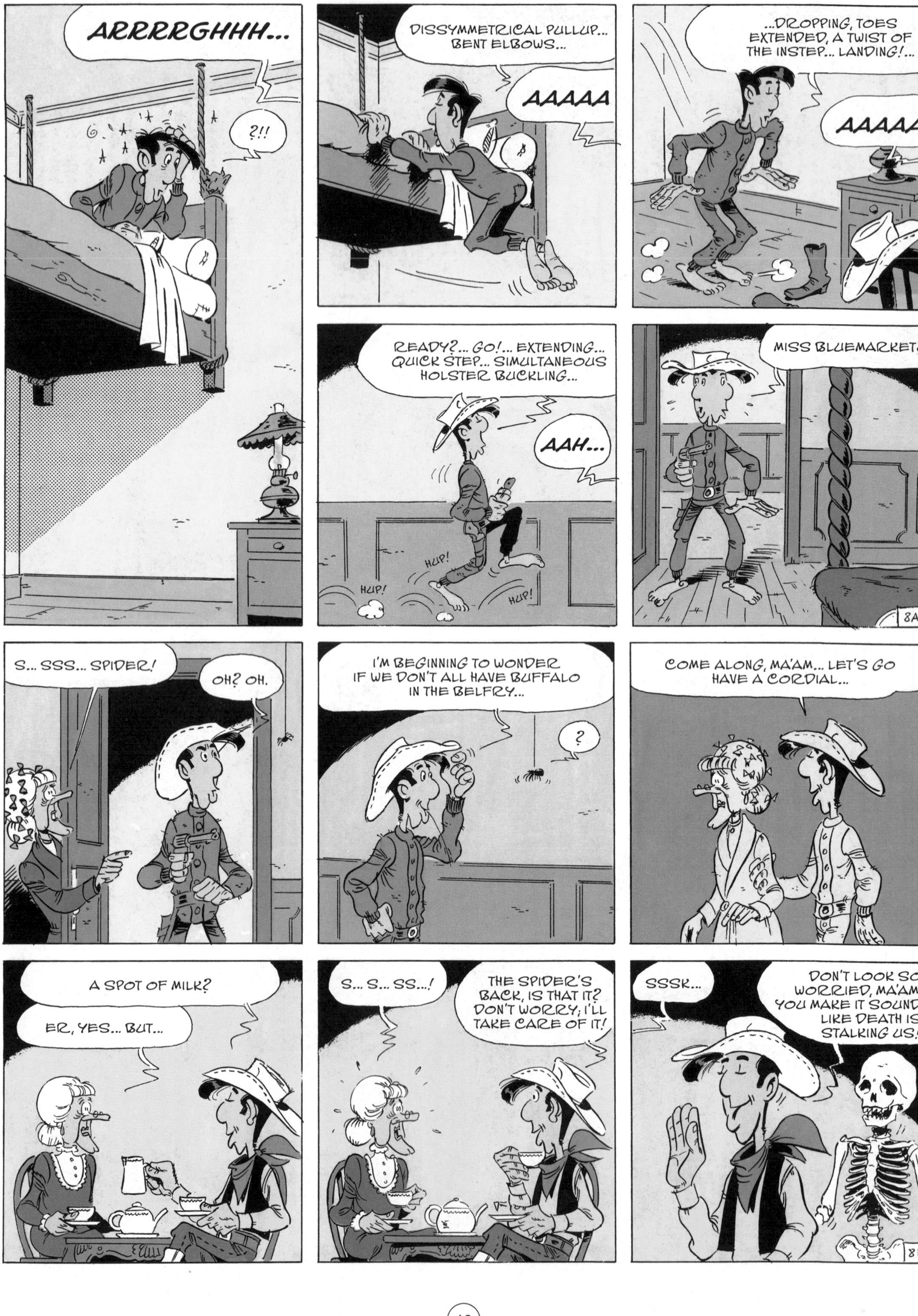
ARRRRGHHH...
?!!
DISSYMMETRICAL PULLUP... BENT ELBOWS...
AAAAA
...DROPPING, TOES EXTENDED, A TWIST OF THE INSTEP... LANDING!...
AAAAA
READY?... GO!... EXTENDING... QUICK STEP... SIMULTANEOUS HOLSTER BUCKLING...
AAH...
HUP!
HUP!
HUP!
MISS BLUEMARKET?
8A
S... SSS... SPIDER!
OH? OH.
I'M BEGINNING TO WONDER IF WE DON'T ALL HAVE BUFFALO IN THE BELFRY...
?
COME ALONG, MA'AM... LET'S GO HAVE A CORDIAL...
A SPOT OF MILK?
ER, YES... BUT...
S... S... SS...!
THE SPIDER'S BACK, IS THAT IT? DON'T WORRY; I'LL TAKE CARE OF IT!
SSSK...
DON'T LOOK SO WORRIED, MA'AM. YOU MAKE IT SOUND LIKE DEATH IS STALKING US!
8B

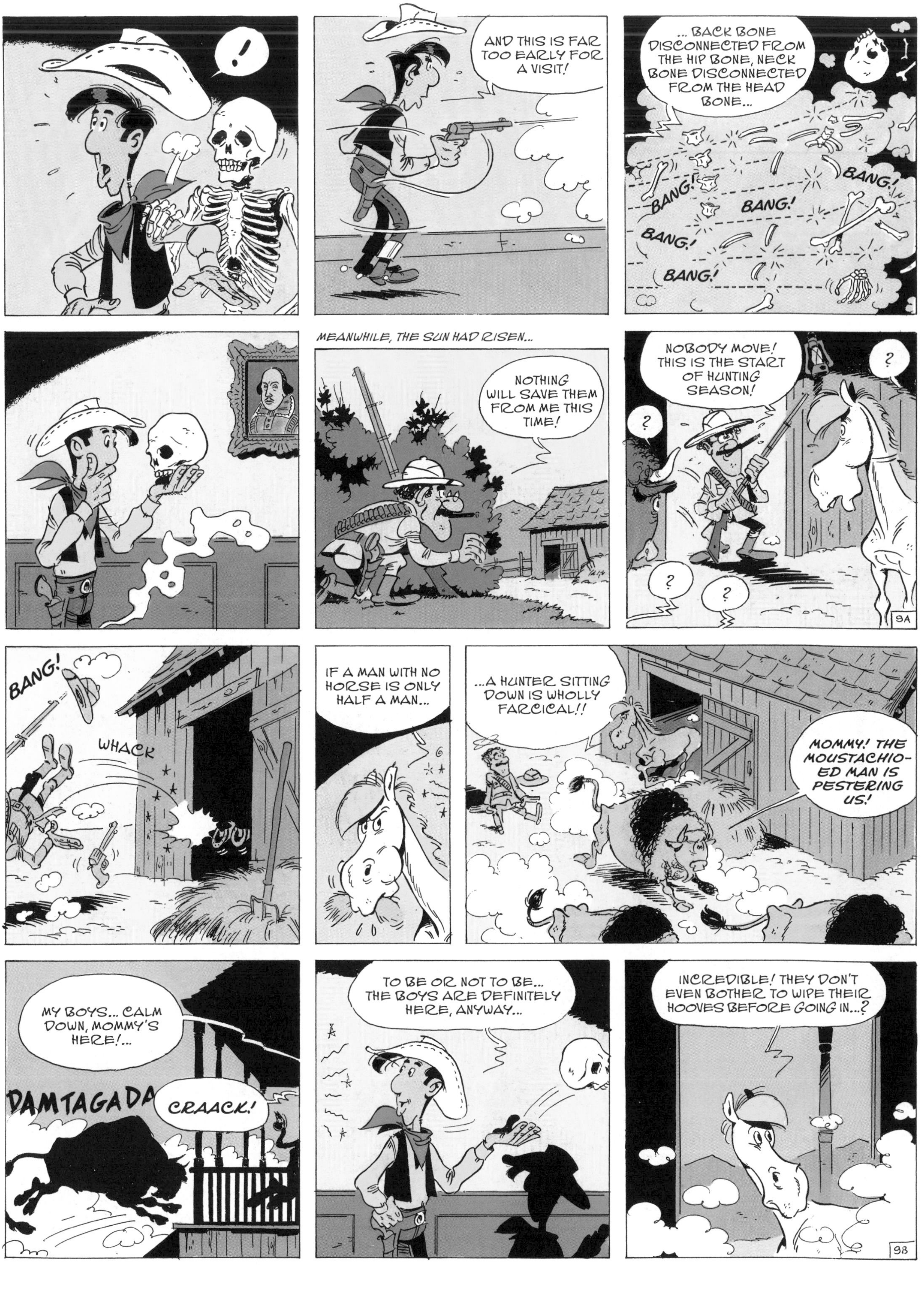
!
AND THIS IS FAR TOO EARLY FOR A VISIT!
... BACK BONE DISCONNECTED FROM THE HIP BONE, NECK BONE DISCONNECTED FROM THE HEAD BONE...
BANG!
BANG!
BANG!
BANG!
BANG!
MEANWHILE, THE SUN HAD RISEN...
NOTHING WILL SAVE THEM FROM ME THIS TIME!
NOBODY MOVE! THIS IS THE START OF HUNTING SEASON!
?
?
?
?
9A
BANG!
WHACK
IF A MAN WITH NO HORSE IS ONLY HALF A MAN...
...A HUNTER SITTING DOWN IS WHOLLY FARCICAL!!
MOMMY! THE MOUSTACHIOED MAN IS PESTERING US!
MY BOYS... CALM DOWN, MOMMY'S HERE!...
DAMTAGADA
CRAACK!
TO BE OR NOT TO BE... THE BOYS ARE DEFINITELY HERE, ANYWAY...
INCREDIBLE! THEY DON'T EVEN BOTHER TO WIPE THEIR HOOVES BEFORE GOING IN...?
9B

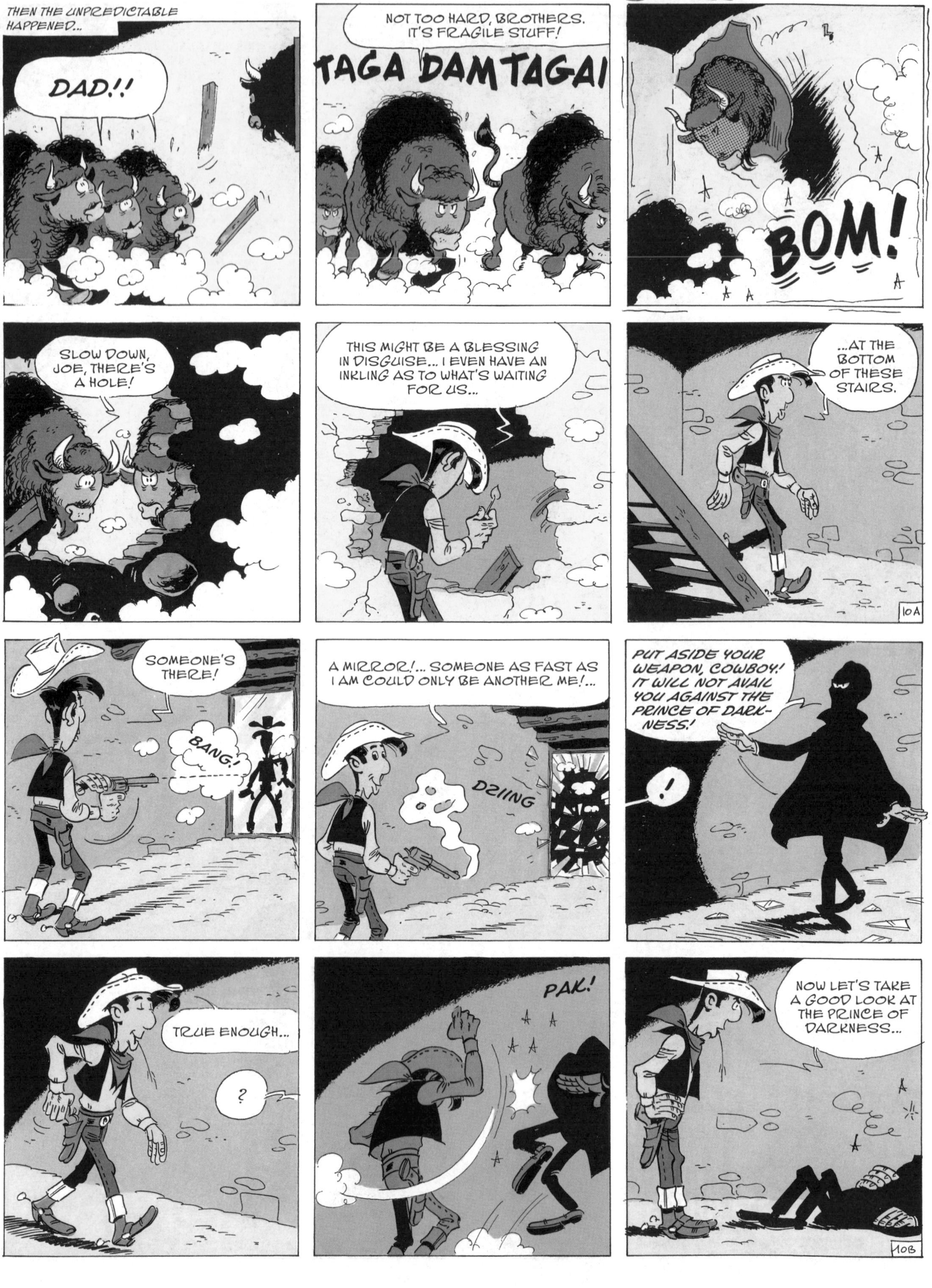
THEN THE UNPREDICTABLE HAPPENED...
DAD!!
NOT TOO HARD, BROTHERS. IT'S FRAGILE STUFF!
TAGA DAM TAGAI
BOM!
SLOW DOWN, JOE, THERE'S A HOLE!
THIS MIGHT BE A BLESSING IN DISGUISE... I EVEN HAVE AN INKLING AS TO WHAT'S WAITING FOR US...
...AT THE BOTTOM OF THESE STAIRS.
10A
SOMEONE'S THERE!
BANG!
A MIRROR!... SOMEONE AS FAST AS I AM COULD ONLY BE ANOTHER ME!...
DZIING
PUT ASIDE YOUR WEAPON, COWBOY! IT WILL NOT AVAIL YOU AGAINST THE PRINCE OF DARKNESS!
!
TRUE ENOUGH...
?
PAK!
NOW LET'S TAKE A GOOD LOOK AT THE PRINCE OF DARKNESS...
10B

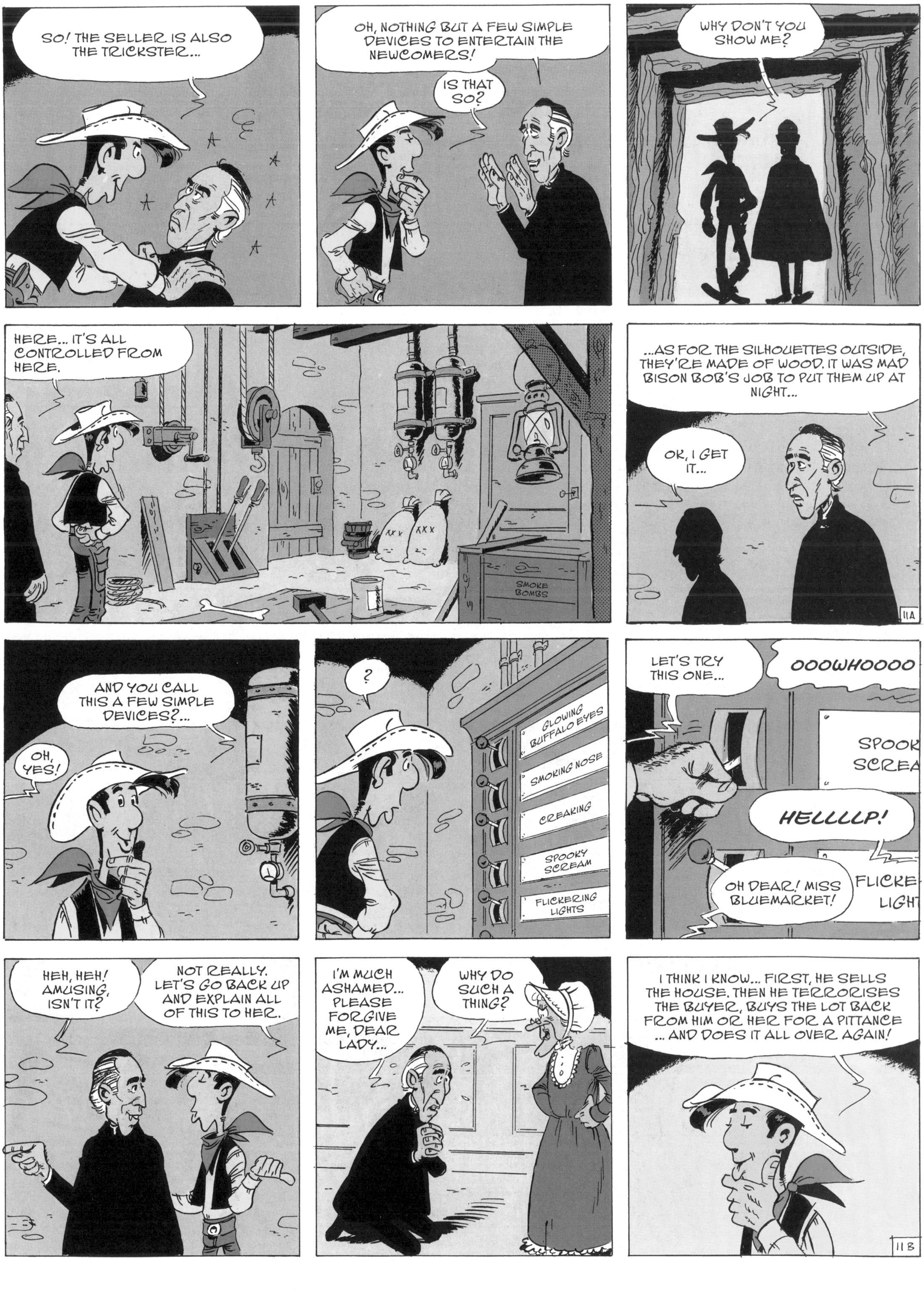
SO! THE SELLER IS ALSO THE TRICKSTER...
OH, NOTHING BUT A FEW SIMPLE DEVICES TO ENTERTAIN THE NEWCOMERS!
IS THAT SO?
WHY DON'T YOU SHOW ME?
HERE... IT'S ALL CONTROLLED FROM HERE.
SMOKE BOMBS
...AS FOR THE SILHOUETTES OUTSIDE, THEY'RE MADE OF WOOD. IT WAS MAD BISON BOB'S JOB TO PUT THEM UP AT NIGHT...
OK, I GET IT...
11A
AND YOU CALL THIS A FEW SIMPLE DEVICES?...
OH, YES!
?
GLOWING BUFFALO EYES
SMOKING NOSE
CREAKING
SPOOKY SCREAM
FLICKERING LIGHTS
LET'S TRY THIS ONE...
OOOWHOOOO
HELLLLP!
OH DEAR! MISS BLUEMARKET!
HEH, HEH! AMUSING, ISN'T IT?
NOT REALLY. LET'S GO BACK UP AND EXPLAIN ALL OF THIS TO HER.
I'M MUCH ASHAMED... PLEASE FORGIVE ME, DEAR LADY...
WHY DO SUCH A THING?
I THINK I KNOW... FIRST, HE SELLS THE HOUSE. THEN HE TERRORISES THE BUYER, BUYS THE LOT BACK FROM HIM OR HER FOR A PITTANCE ... AND DOES IT ALL OVER AGAIN!
11B

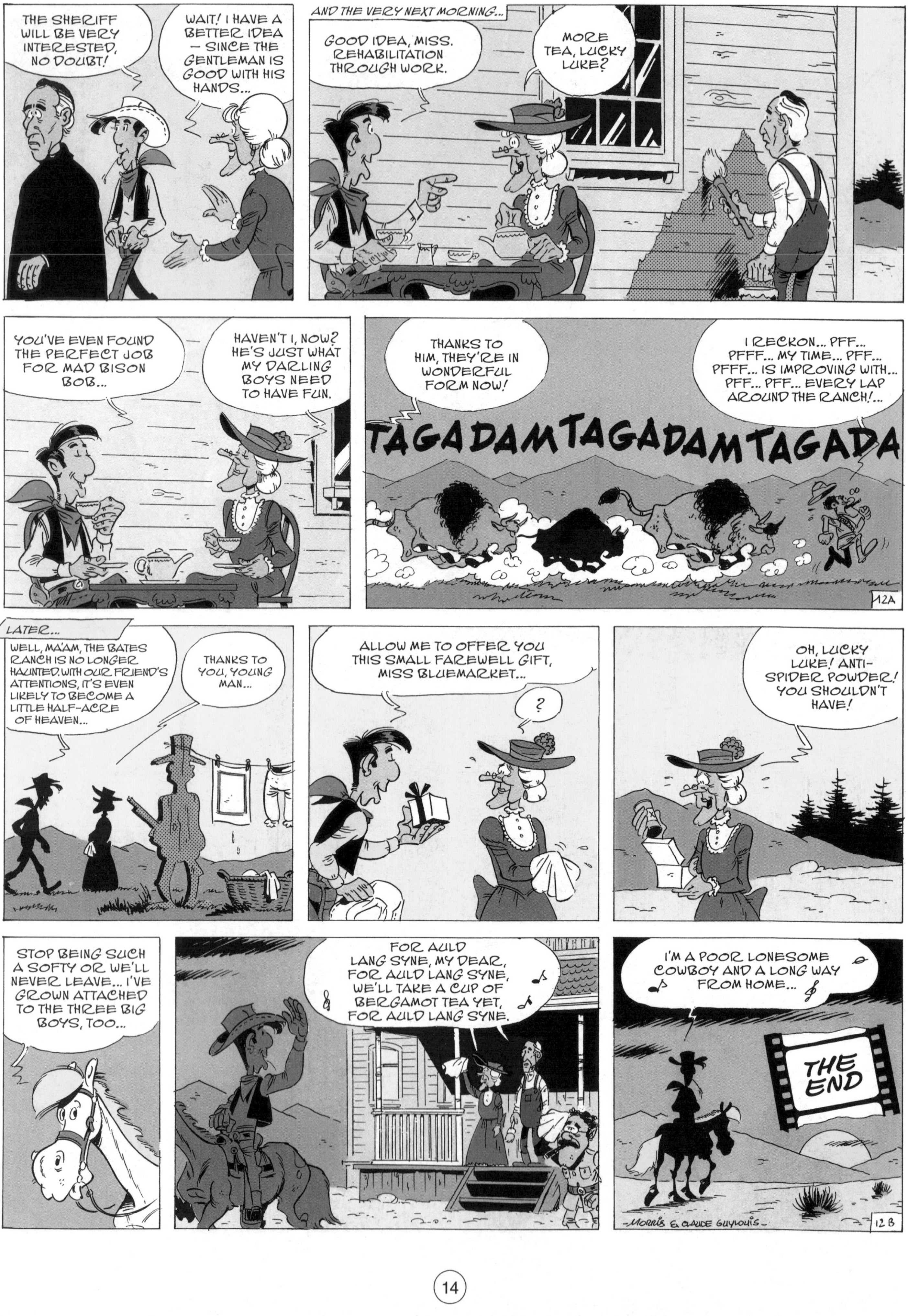

THE SHERIFF WILL BE VERY INTERESTED, NO DOUBT!
WAIT! I HAVE A BETTER IDEA — SINCE THE GENTLEMAN IS GOOD WITH HIS HANDS...
AND THE VERY NEXT MORNING...
GOOD IDEA, MISS. REHABILITATION THROUGH WORK.
MORE TEA, LUCKY LUKE?
YOU'VE EVEN FOUND THE PERFECT JOB FOR MAD BISON BOB...
HAVEN'T I, NOW? HE'S JUST WHAT MY DARLING BOYS NEED TO HAVE FUN.
THANKS TO HIM, THEY'RE IN WONDERFUL FORM NOW!
I RECKON... PFF... PFFF... MY TIME... PFF... PFFF... IS IMPROVING WITH... PFF... PFF... EVERY LAP AROUND THE RANCH!...
TAGADAMTAGADAMTAGADA
12A
LATER...
WELL, MA'AM, THE BATES RANCH IS NO LONGER HAUNTED. WITH OUR FRIEND'S ATTENTIONS, IT'S EVEN LIKELY TO BECOME A LITTLE HALF-ACRE OF HEAVEN...
THANKS TO YOU, YOUNG MAN...
ALLOW ME TO OFFER YOU THIS SMALL FAREWELL GIFT, MISS BLUEMARKET...
?
OH, LUCKY LUKE! ANTI-SPIDER POWDER! YOU SHOULDN'T HAVE!
STOP BEING SUCH A SOFTY OR WE'LL NEVER LEAVE... I'VE GROWN ATTACHED TO THE THREE BIG BOYS, TOO...
FOR AULD LANG SYNE, MY DEAR, FOR AULD LANG SYNE, WE'LL TAKE A CUP OF BERGAMOT TEA YET, FOR AULD LANG SYNE.
I'M A POOR LONESOME COWBOY AND A LONG WAY FROM HOME...
THE END
-MORRIS & CLAUDE GUYLOUIS-
12 B

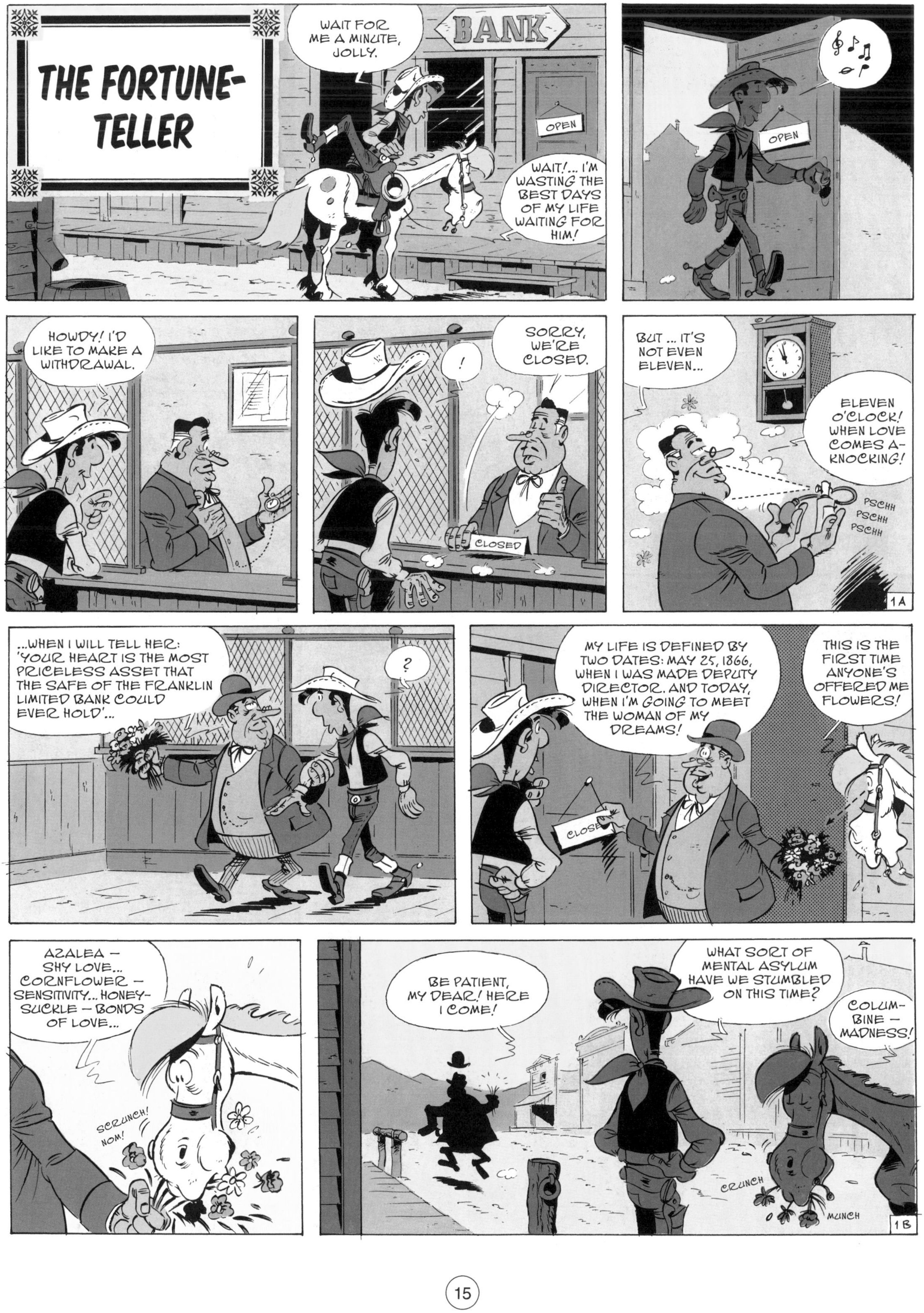
THE FORTUNE-TELLER
BANK
WAIT FOR ME A MINUTE, JOLLY.
OPEN
WAIT!... I'M WASTING THE BEST DAYS OF MY LIFE WAITING FOR HIM!
OPEN
HOWDY! I'D LIKE TO MAKE A WITHDRAWAL.
!
SORRY, WE'RE CLOSED.
CLOSED
BUT ... IT'S NOT EVEN ELEVEN...
ELEVEN O'CLOCK! WHEN LOVE COMES A-KNOCKING!
PSCHH PSCHH PSCHH
1A
...WHEN I WILL TELL HER: 'YOUR HEART IS THE MOST PRICELESS ASSET THAT THE SAFE OF THE FRANKLIN LIMITED BANK COULD EVER HOLD'...
?
MY LIFE IS DEFINED BY TWO DATES: MAY 25, 1866, WHEN I WAS MADE DEPUTY DIRECTOR. AND TODAY, WHEN I'M GOING TO MEET THE WOMAN OF MY DREAMS!
THIS IS THE FIRST TIME ANYONE'S OFFERED ME FLOWERS!
AZALEA – SHY LOVE... CORNFLOWER – SENSITIVITY... HONEYSUCKLE – BONDS OF LOVE...
SCRUNCH! NOM!
BE PATIENT, MY DEAR! HERE I COME!
WHAT SORT OF MENTAL ASYLUM HAVE WE STUMBLED ON THIS TIME?
COLUMBINE – MADNESS!
CRUNCH
MUNCH
1B

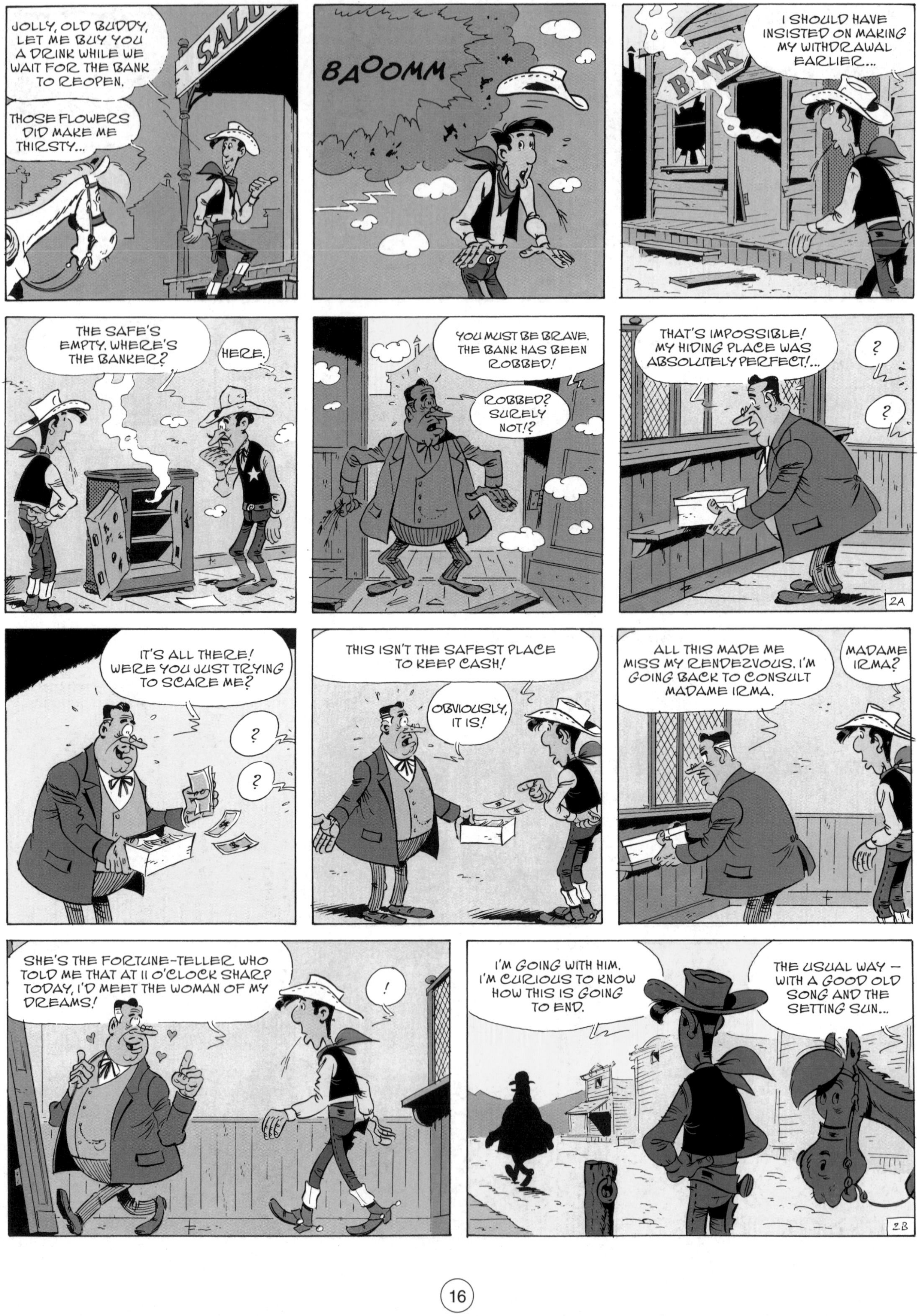
JOLLY, OLD BUDDY, LET ME BUY YOU A DRINK WHILE WE WAIT FOR THE BANK TO REOPEN.
THOSE FLOWERS DID MAKE ME THIRSTY...
BAOOMM
I SHOULD HAVE INSISTED ON MAKING MY WITHDRAWAL EARLIER...
THE SAFE'S EMPTY. WHERE'S THE BANKER?
HERE.
YOU MUST BE BRAVE. THE BANK HAS BEEN ROBBED!
ROBBED? SURELY NOT!?
THAT'S IMPOSSIBLE! MY HIDING PLACE WAS ABSOLUTELY PERFECT!...
?
?
2A
IT'S ALL THERE! WERE YOU JUST TRYING TO SCARE ME?
?
?
THIS ISN'T THE SAFEST PLACE TO KEEP CASH!
OBVIOUSLY, IT IS!
ALL THIS MADE ME MISS MY RENDEZVOUS. I'M GOING BACK TO CONSULT MADAME IRMA.
MADAME IRMA?
SHE'S THE FORTUNE-TELLER WHO TOLD ME THAT AT 11 O'CLOCK SHARP TODAY, I'D MEET THE WOMAN OF MY DREAMS!
!
I'M GOING WITH HIM. I'M CURIOUS TO KNOW HOW THIS IS GOING TO END.
THE USUAL WAY — WITH A GOOD OLD SONG AND THE SETTING SUN...
2B

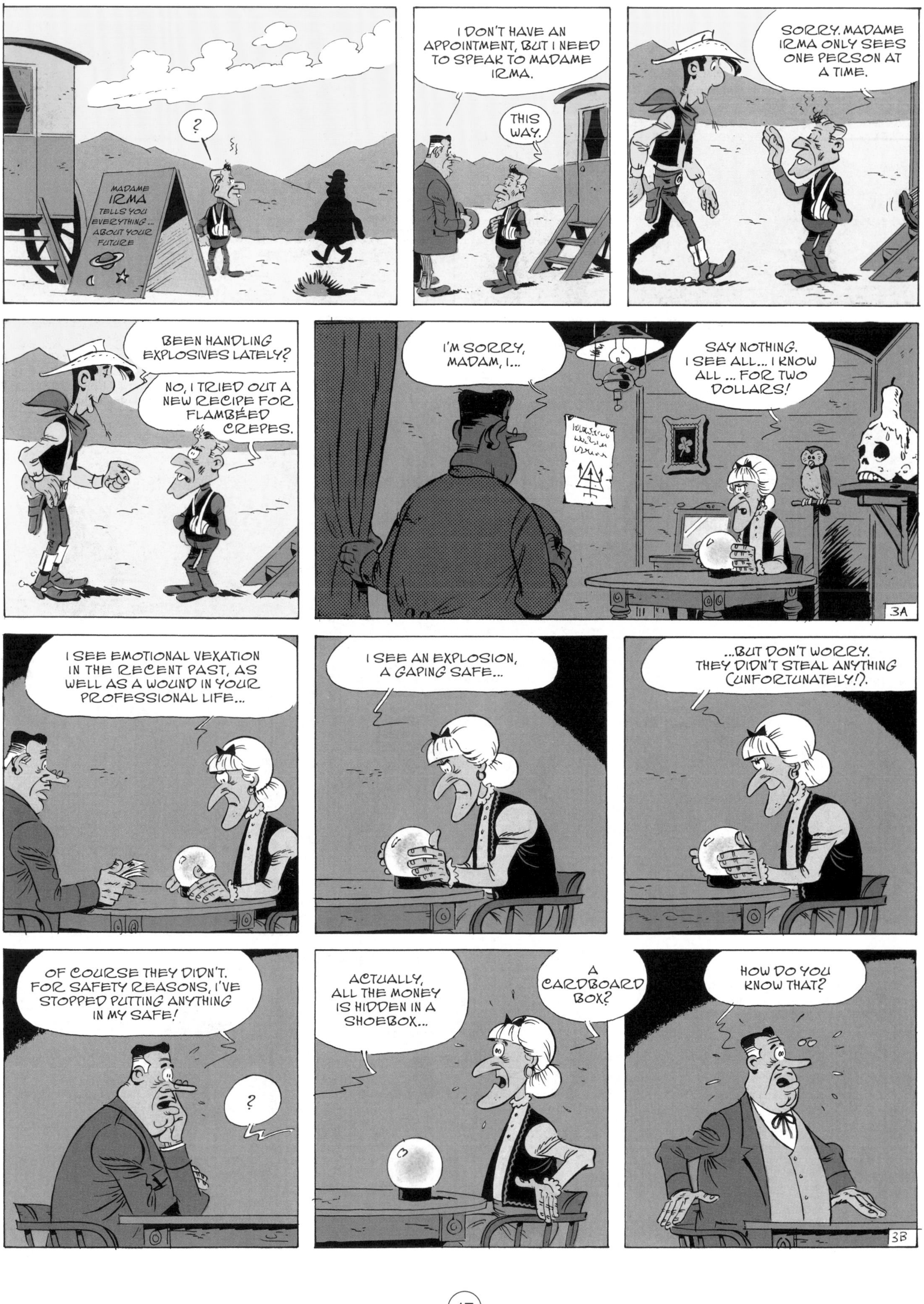
MADAME IRMA TELLS YOU EVERYTHING... ABOUT YOUR FUTURE
?
I DON'T HAVE AN APPOINTMENT, BUT I NEED TO SPEAK TO MADAME IRMA.
THIS WAY.
SORRY. MADAME IRMA ONLY SEES ONE PERSON AT A TIME.
BEEN HANDLING EXPLOSIVES LATELY?
NO, I TRIED OUT A NEW RECIPE FOR FLAMBÉED CREPES.
I'M SORRY, MADAM, I...
SAY NOTHING. I SEE ALL... I KNOW ALL ... FOR TWO DOLLARS!
3A
I SEE EMOTIONAL VEXATION IN THE RECENT PAST, AS WELL AS A WOUND IN YOUR PROFESSIONAL LIFE...
I SEE AN EXPLOSION, A GAPING SAFE...
...BUT DON'T WORRY. THEY DIDN'T STEAL ANYTHING (UNFORTUNATELY!).
OF COURSE THEY DIDN'T. FOR SAFETY REASONS, I'VE STOPPED PUTTING ANYTHING IN MY SAFE!
?
ACTUALLY, ALL THE MONEY IS HIDDEN IN A SHOEBOX...
A CARDBOARD BOX?
HOW DO YOU KNOW THAT?
3B

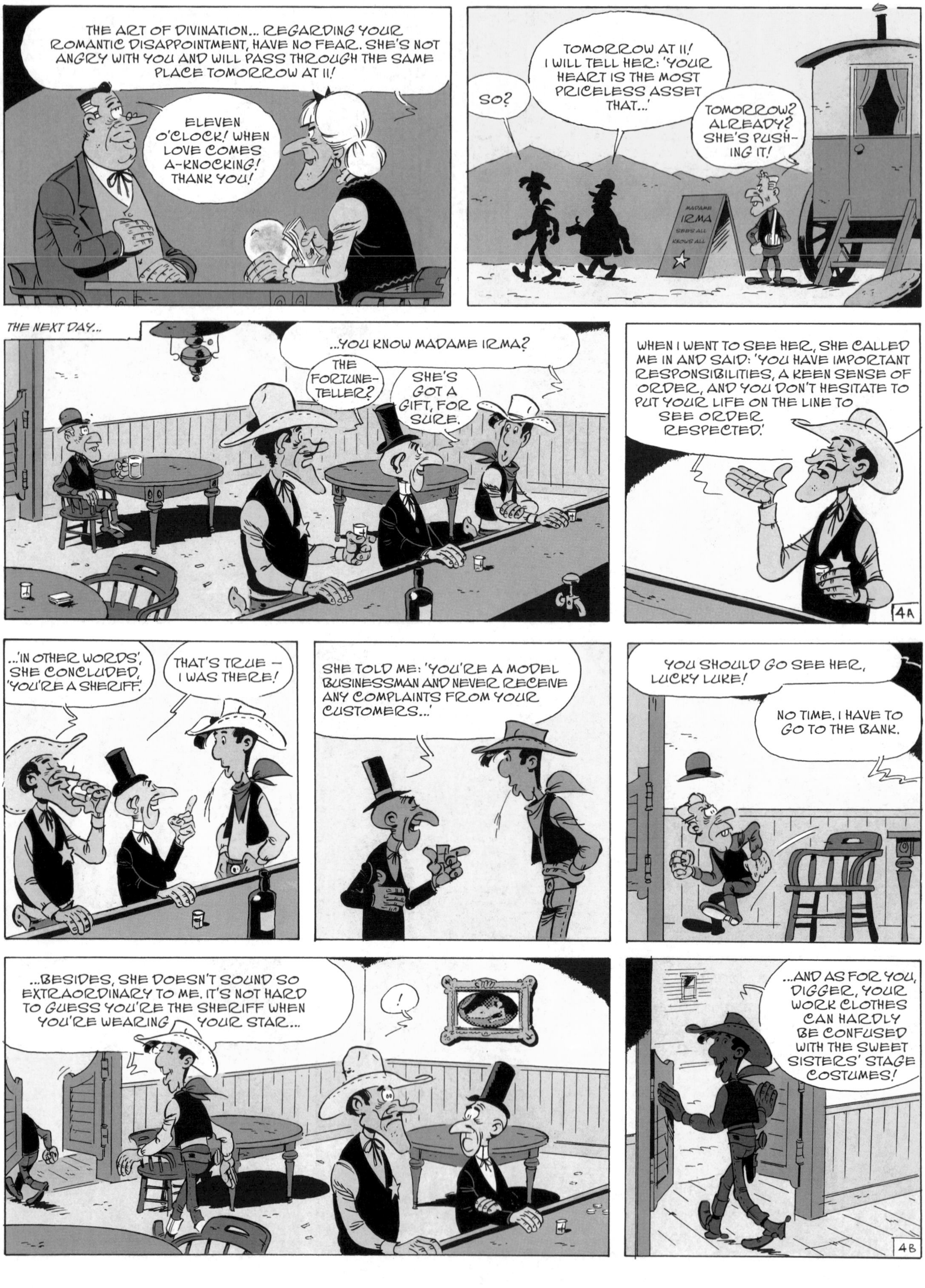
THE ART OF DIVINATION... REGARDING YOUR ROMANTIC DISAPPOINTMENT, HAVE NO FEAR. SHE'S NOT ANGRY WITH YOU AND WILL PASS THROUGH THE SAME PLACE TOMORROW AT 11!
ELEVEN O'CLOCK! WHEN LOVE COMES A-KNOCKING! THANK YOU!
SO?
TOMORROW AT 11! I WILL TELL HER: 'YOUR HEART IS THE MOST PRICELESS ASSET THAT...'
TOMORROW? ALREADY? SHE'S PUSHING IT!
MADAME IRMA
THE NEXT DAY...
...YOU KNOW MADAME IRMA?
THE FORTUNE-TELLER?
SHE'S GOT A GIFT, FOR SURE.
WHEN I WENT TO SEE HER, SHE CALLED ME IN AND SAID: 'YOU HAVE IMPORTANT RESPONSIBILITIES, A KEEN SENSE OF ORDER, AND YOU DON'T HESITATE TO PUT YOUR LIFE ON THE LINE TO SEE ORDER RESPECTED.'
4A
...'IN OTHER WORDS', SHE CONCLUDED, 'YOU'RE A SHERIFF.'
THAT'S TRUE – I WAS THERE!
SHE TOLD ME: 'YOU'RE A MODEL BUSINESSMAN AND NEVER RECEIVE ANY COMPLAINTS FROM YOUR CUSTOMERS...'
YOU SHOULD GO SEE HER, LUCKY LUKE!
NO TIME. I HAVE TO GO TO THE BANK.
...BESIDES, SHE DOESN'T SOUND SO EXTRAORDINARY TO ME. IT'S NOT HARD TO GUESS YOU'RE THE SHERIFF WHEN YOU'RE WEARING YOUR STAR...
!
...AND AS FOR YOU, DIGGER, YOUR WORK CLOTHES CAN HARDLY BE CONFUSED WITH THE SWEET SISTERS' STAGE COSTUMES!
4B

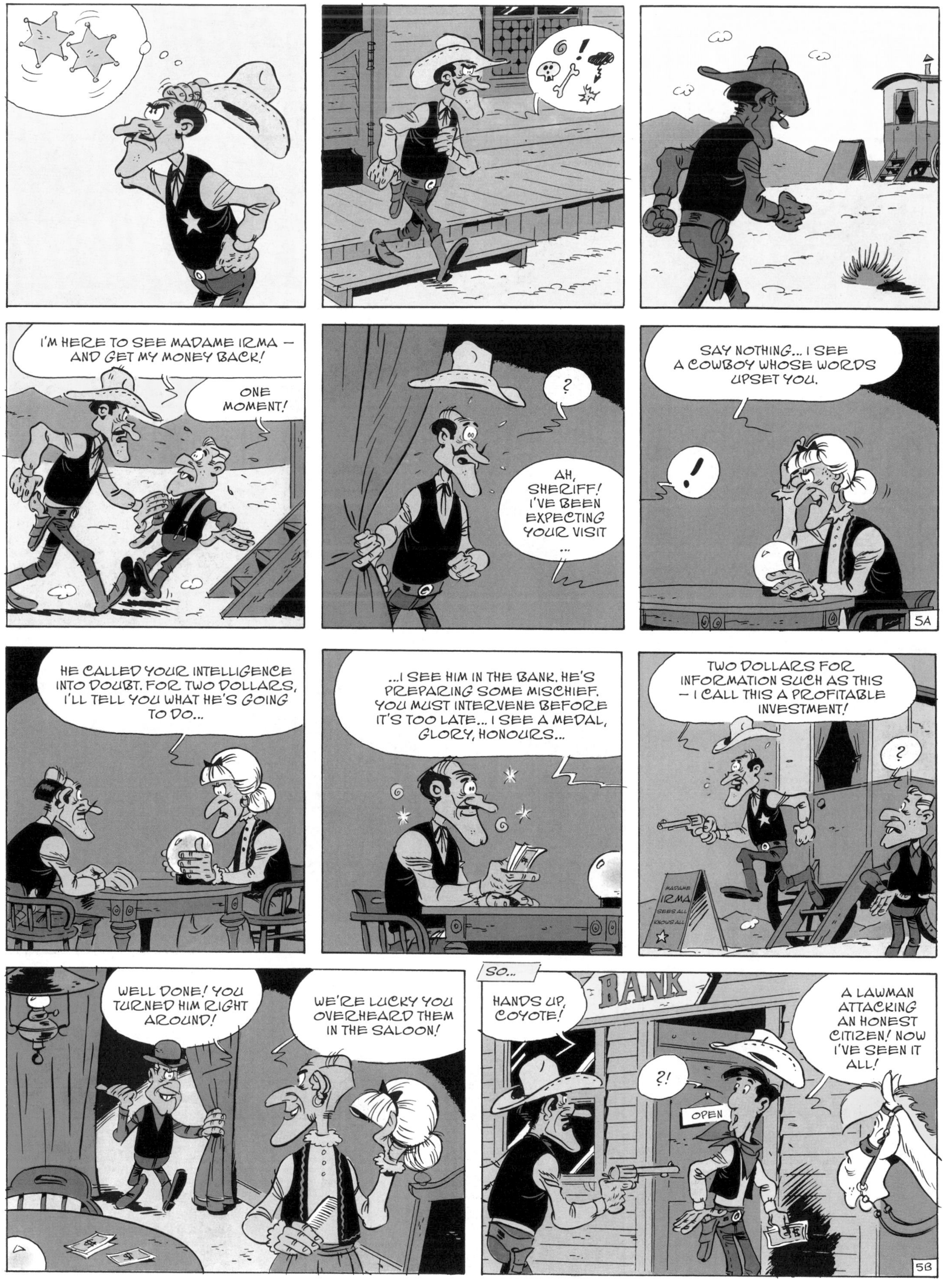
I'M HERE TO SEE MADAME IRMA — AND GET MY MONEY BACK!
ONE MOMENT!
?
AH, SHERIFF! I'VE BEEN EXPECTING YOUR VISIT ...
SAY NOTHING... I SEE A COWBOY WHOSE WORDS UPSET YOU.
!
5A
HE CALLED YOUR INTELLIGENCE INTO DOUBT. FOR TWO DOLLARS, I'LL TELL YOU WHAT HE'S GOING TO DO...
...I SEE HIM IN THE BANK. HE'S PREPARING SOME MISCHIEF. YOU MUST INTERVENE BEFORE IT'S TOO LATE... I SEE A MEDAL, GLORY, HONOURS...
TWO DOLLARS FOR INFORMATION SUCH AS THIS — I CALL THIS A PROFITABLE INVESTMENT!
?
MADAME IRMA SEES ALL KNOWS ALL
WELL DONE! YOU TURNED HIM RIGHT AROUND!
WE'RE LUCKY YOU OVERHEARD THEM IN THE SALOON!
SO...
BANK
HANDS UP, COYOTE!
?!
OPEN
A LAWMAN ATTACKING AN HONEST CITIZEN! NOW I'VE SEEN IT ALL!
5B

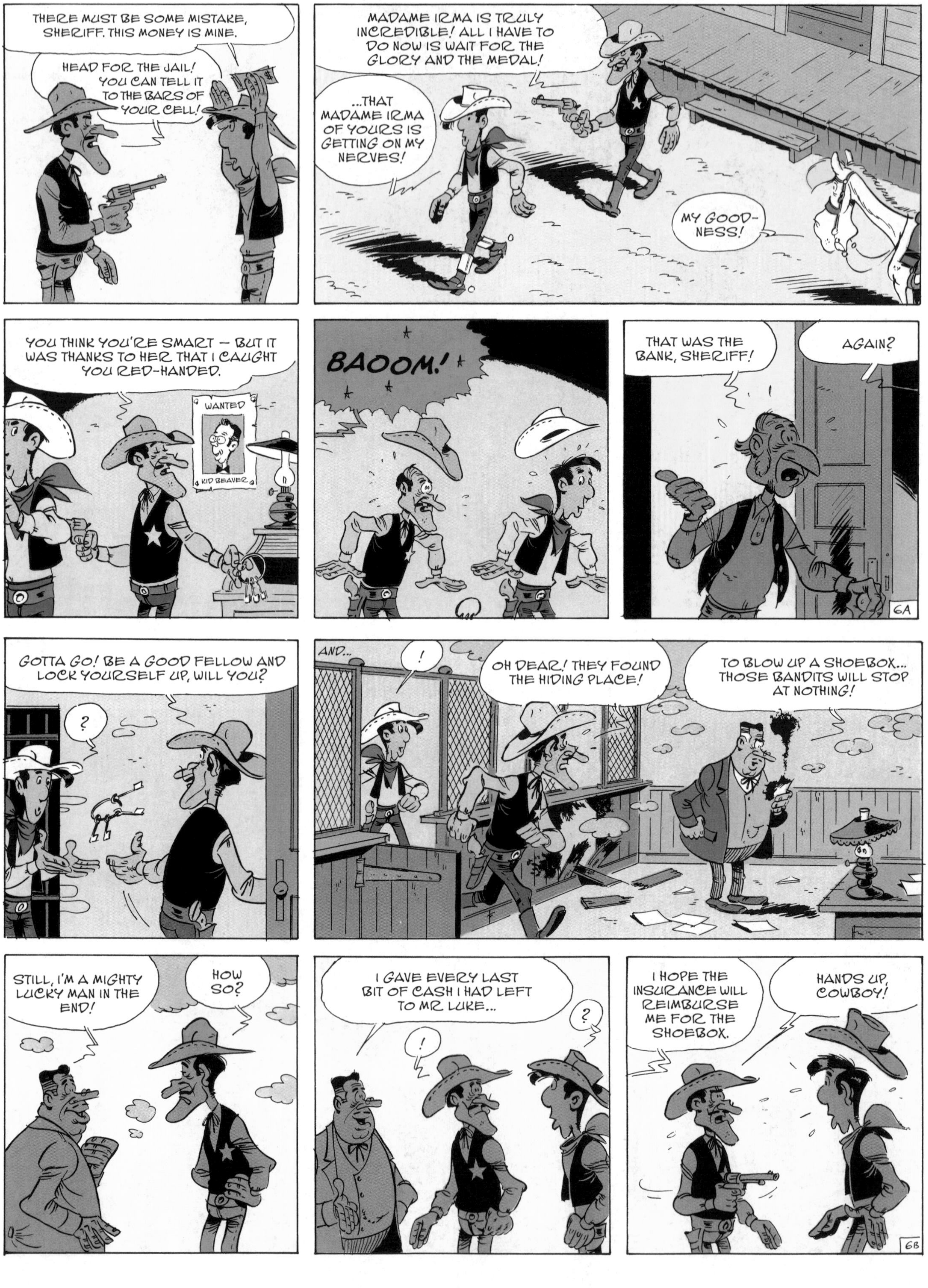
THERE MUST BE SOME MISTAKE, SHERIFF. THIS MONEY IS MINE.
HEAD FOR THE JAIL! YOU CAN TELL IT TO THE BARS OF YOUR CELL!
MADAME IRMA IS TRULY INCREDIBLE! ALL I HAVE TO DO NOW IS WAIT FOR THE GLORY AND THE MEDAL!
...THAT MADAME IRMA OF YOURS IS GETTING ON MY NERVES!
MY GOOD-NESS!
YOU THINK YOU'RE SMART — BUT IT WAS THANKS TO HER THAT I CAUGHT YOU RED-HANDED.
WANTED
KID BEAVER
BAOOM!
THAT WAS THE BANK, SHERIFF!
AGAIN?
6A
GOTTA GO! BE A GOOD FELLOW AND LOCK YOURSELF UP, WILL YOU?
?
AND...
!
OH DEAR! THEY FOUND THE HIDING PLACE!
TO BLOW UP A SHOEBOX... THOSE BANDITS WILL STOP AT NOTHING!
STILL, I'M A MIGHTY LUCKY MAN IN THE END!
HOW SO?
I GAVE EVERY LAST BIT OF CASH I HAD LEFT TO MR LUKE...
!
?
I HOPE THE INSURANCE WILL REIMBURSE ME FOR THE SHOEBOX.
HANDS UP, COWBOY!
6B

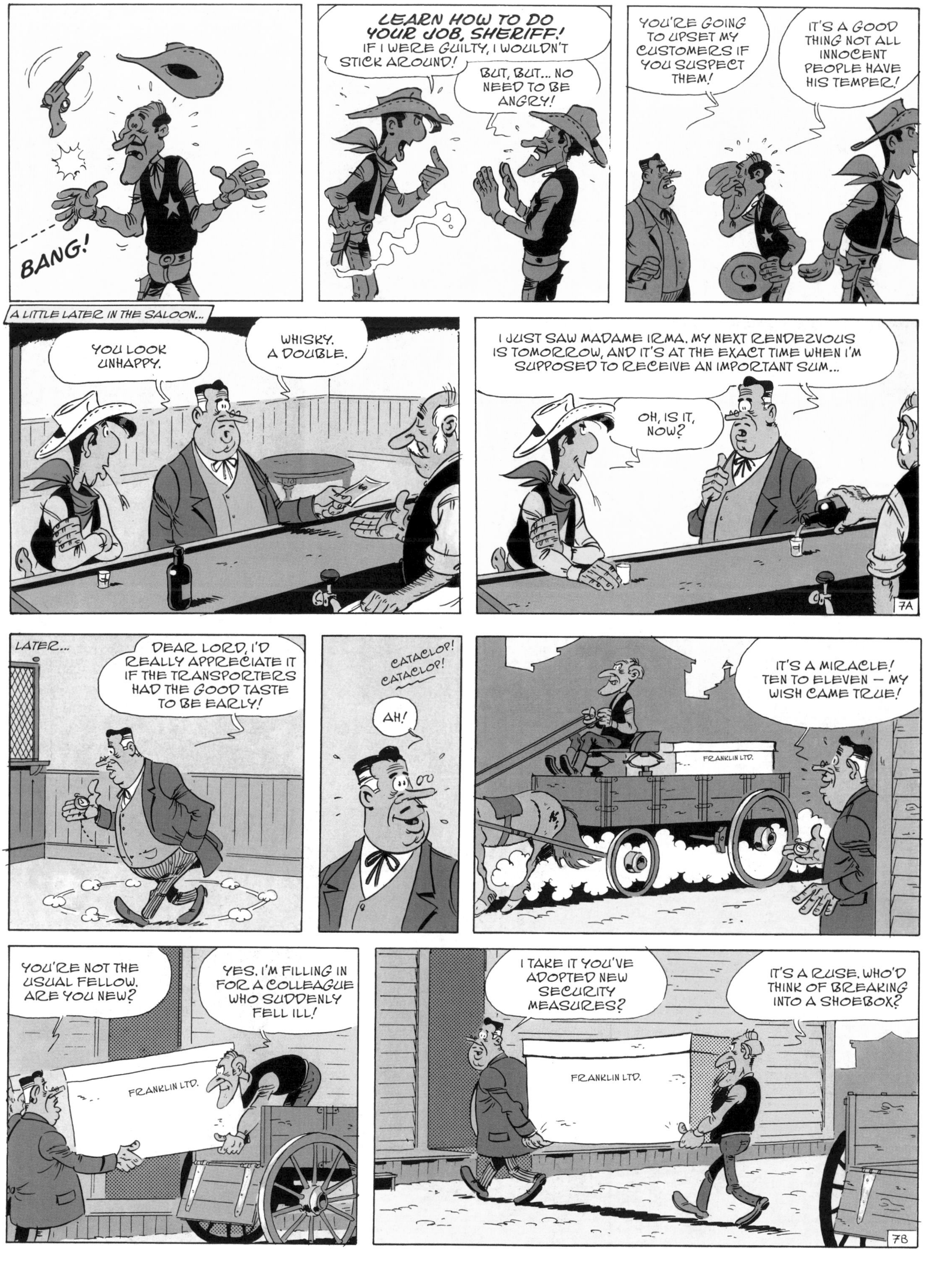
BANG!
LEARN HOW TO DO YOUR JOB, SHERIFF! IF I WERE GUILTY, I WOULDN'T STICK AROUND!
BUT, BUT... NO NEED TO BE ANGRY!
YOU'RE GOING TO UPSET MY CUSTOMERS IF YOU SUSPECT THEM!
IT'S A GOOD THING NOT ALL INNOCENT PEOPLE HAVE HIS TEMPER!
A LITTLE LATER IN THE SALOON...
YOU LOOK UNHAPPY.
WHISKY. A DOUBLE.
I JUST SAW MADAME IRMA. MY NEXT RENDEZVOUS IS TOMORROW, AND IT'S AT THE EXACT TIME WHEN I'M SUPPOSED TO RECEIVE AN IMPORTANT SUM...
OH, IS IT, NOW?
7A
LATER...
DEAR LORD, I'D REALLY APPRECIATE IT IF THE TRANSPORTERS HAD THE GOOD TASTE TO BE EARLY!
CATACLOP! CATACLOP!
AH!
FRANKLIN LTD.
IT'S A MIRACLE! TEN TO ELEVEN — MY WISH CAME TRUE!
YOU'RE NOT THE USUAL FELLOW. ARE YOU NEW?
YES. I'M FILLING IN FOR A COLLEAGUE WHO SUDDENLY FELL ILL!
FRANKLIN LTD.
I TAKE IT YOU'VE ADOPTED NEW SECURITY MEASURES?
IT'S A RUSE. WHO'D THINK OF BREAKING INTO A SHOEBOX?
FRANKLIN LTD.
7B

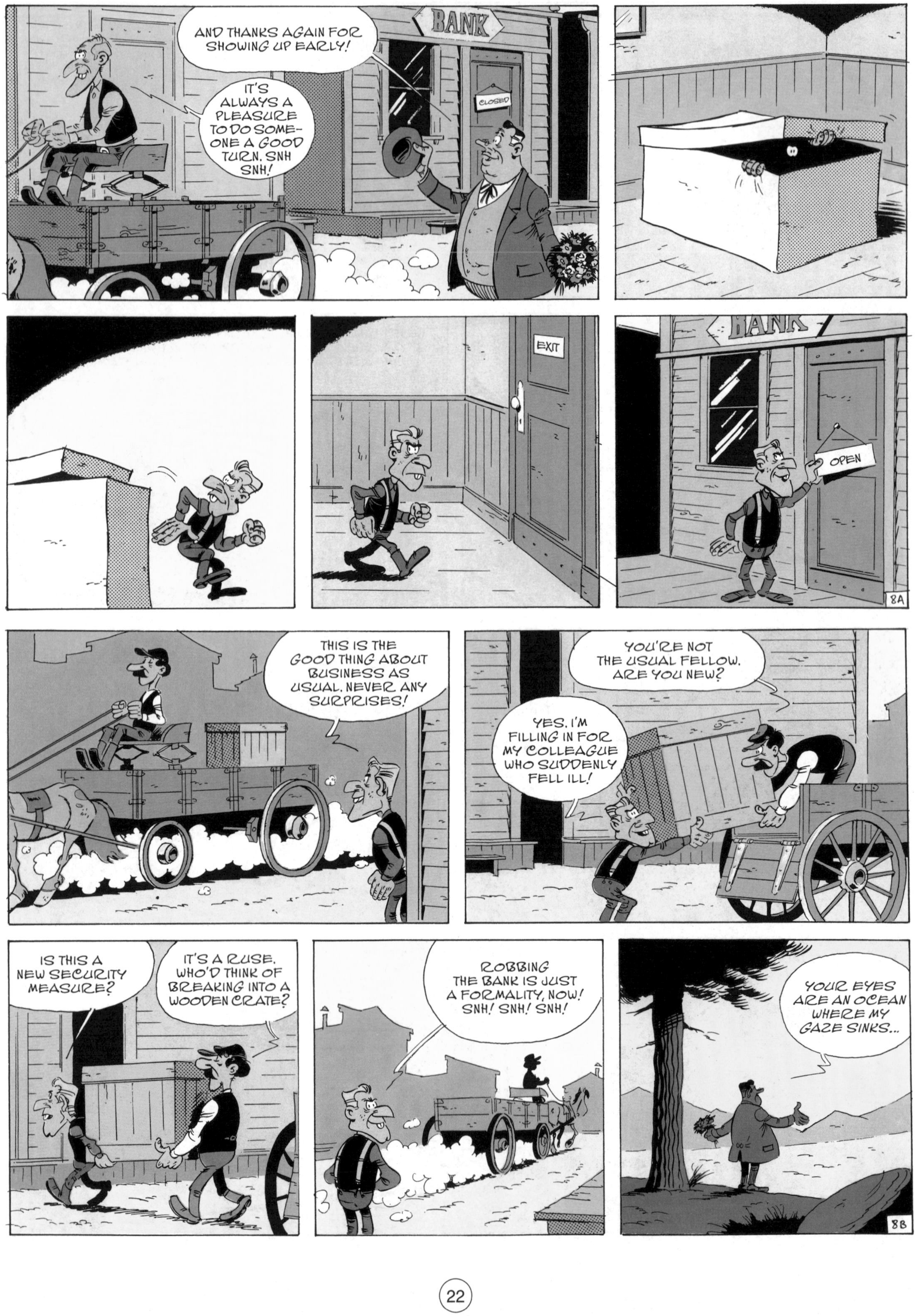
AND THANKS AGAIN FOR SHOWING UP EARLY!
IT'S ALWAYS A PLEASURE TO DO SOME-ONE A GOOD TURN. SNH SNH!
BANK
CLOSED
EXIT
BANK
OPEN
8A
THIS IS THE GOOD THING ABOUT BUSINESS AS USUAL. NEVER ANY SURPRISES!
YOU'RE NOT THE USUAL FELLOW. ARE YOU NEW?
YES. I'M FILLING IN FOR MY COLLEAGUE WHO SUDDENLY FELL ILL!
IS THIS A NEW SECURITY MEASURE?
IT'S A RUSE. WHO'D THINK OF BREAKING INTO A WOODEN CRATE?
ROBBING THE BANK IS JUST A FORMALITY, NOW! SNH! SNH! SNH!
YOUR EYES ARE AN OCEAN WHERE MY GAZE SINKS...
8B

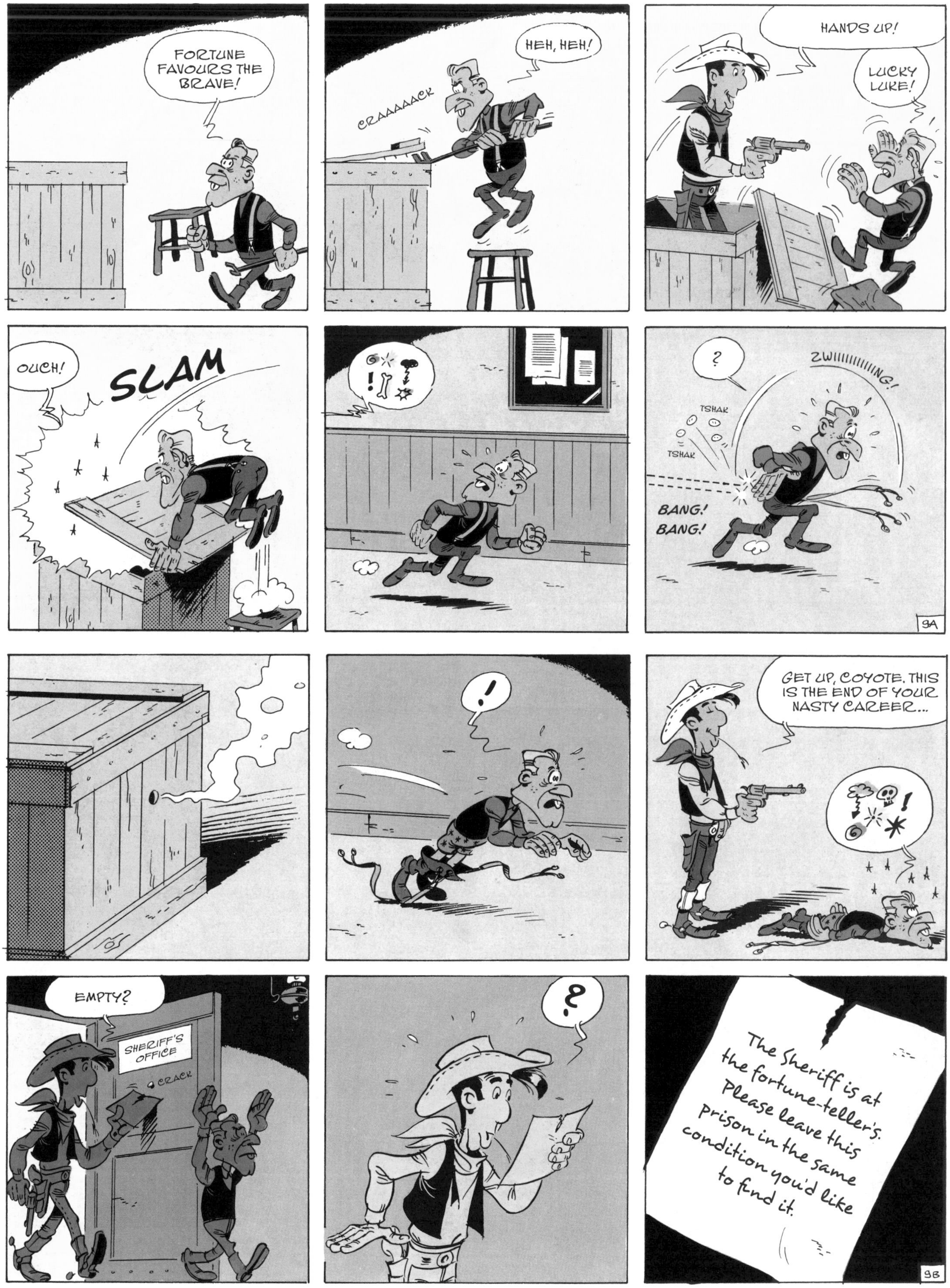

FORTUNE FAVOURS THE BRAVE!
HEH, HEH!
CRAAAAACK
HANDS UP!
LUCKY LUKE!
OUCH!
SLAM
?
ZWIIIIIIIIIING!
TSHAK
TSHAK
BANG! BANG!
9A
!
GET UP, COYOTE. THIS IS THE END OF YOUR NASTY CAREER...
EMPTY?
SHERIFF'S OFFICE
CRACK
?
The Sheriff is at the fortune-teller's. Please leave this prison in the same condition you'd like to find it.
9B

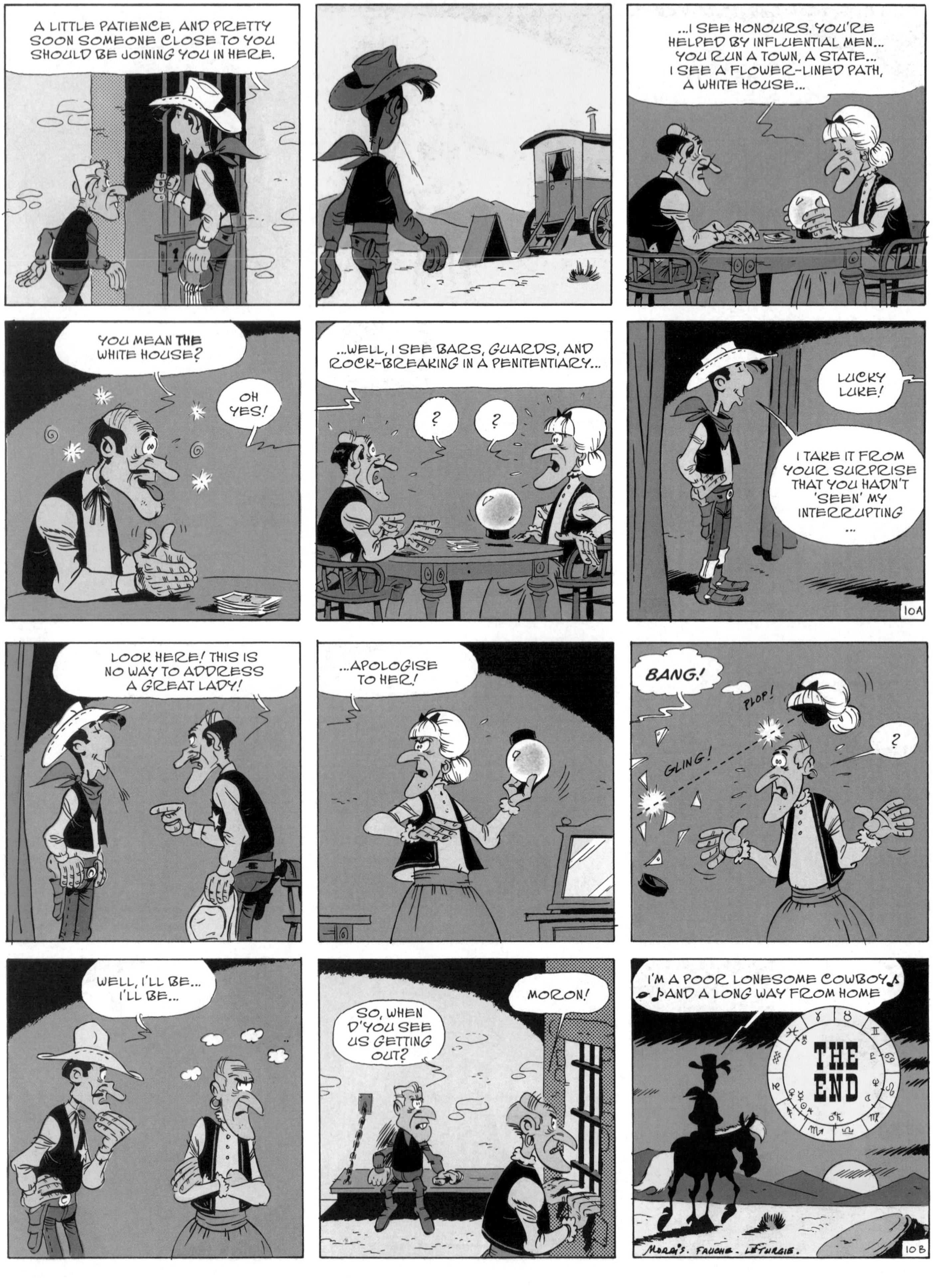
A LITTLE PATIENCE, AND PRETTY SOON SOMEONE CLOSE TO YOU SHOULD BE JOINING YOU IN HERE.
...I SEE HONOURS. YOU'RE HELPED BY INFLUENTIAL MEN... YOU RUN A TOWN, A STATE... I SEE A FLOWER-LINED PATH, A WHITE HOUSE...
YOU MEAN THE WHITE HOUSE?
OH YES!
...WELL, I SEE BARS, GUARDS, AND ROCK-BREAKING IN A PENITENTIARY...
?
?
LUCKY LUKE!
I TAKE IT FROM YOUR SURPRISE THAT YOU HADN'T 'SEEN' MY INTERRUPTING ...
10A
LOOK HERE! THIS IS NO WAY TO ADDRESS A GREAT LADY!
...APOLOGISE TO HER!
BANG!
PLOP!
GLING!
?
WELL, I'LL BE... I'LL BE...
SO, WHEN D'YOU SEE US GETTING OUT?
MORON!
I'M A POOR LONESOME COWBOY AND A LONG WAY FROM HOME
THE END
MORRIS. FAUCHE. LETURGIE.
10B

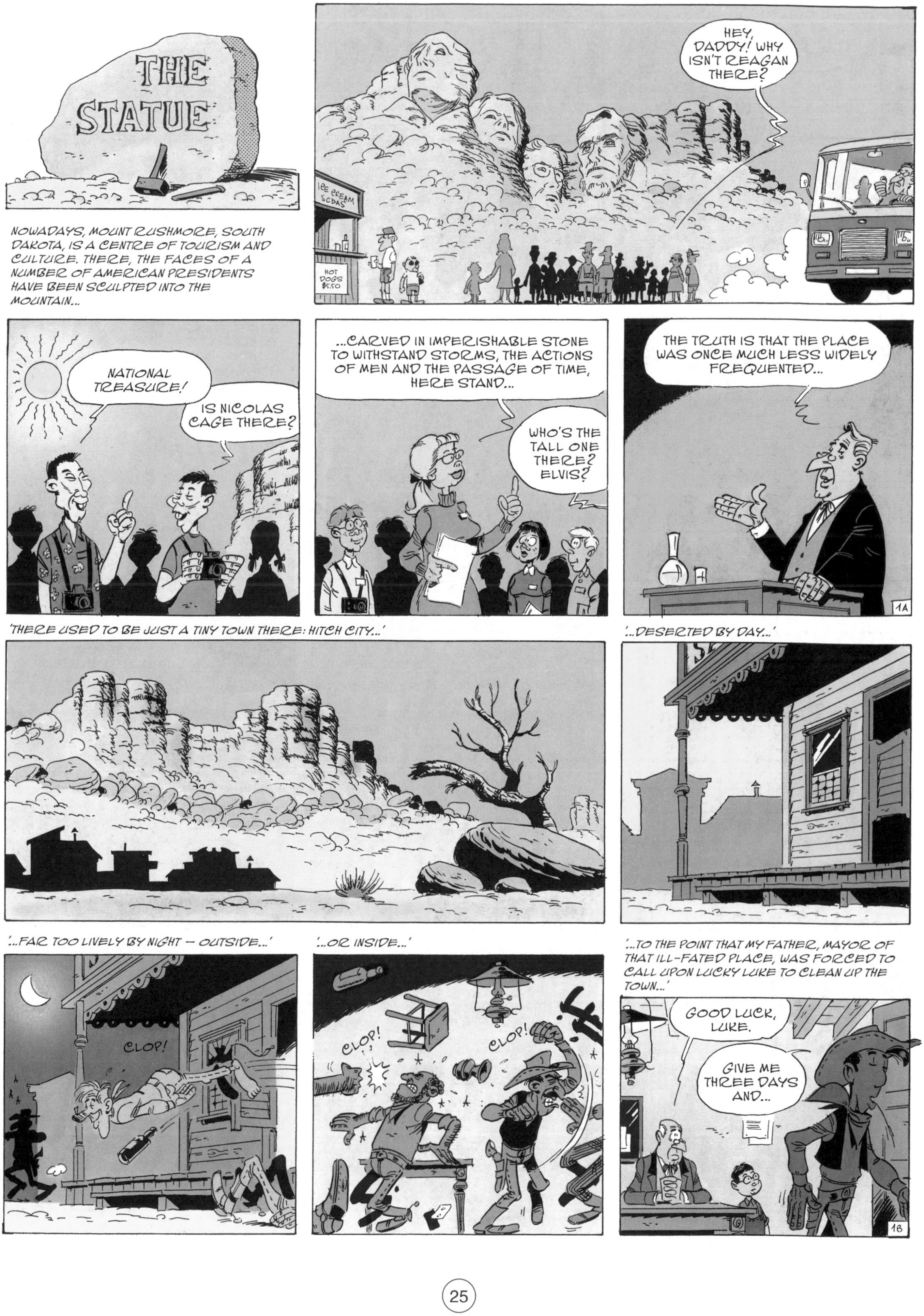
THE STATUE
NOWADAYS, MOUNT RUSHMORE, SOUTH DAKOTA, IS A CENTRE OF TOURISM AND CULTURE. THERE, THE FACES OF A NUMBER OF AMERICAN PRESIDENTS HAVE BEEN SCULPTED INTO THE MOUNTAIN...
ICE CREAM SODAS
HOT DOGS $5.50
HEY, DADDY! WHY ISN'T REAGAN THERE?
NATIONAL TREASURE!
IS NICOLAS CAGE THERE?
...CARVED IN IMPERISHABLE STONE TO WITHSTAND STORMS, THE ACTIONS OF MEN AND THE PASSAGE OF TIME, HERE STAND...
WHO'S THE TALL ONE THERE? ELVIS?
THE TRUTH IS THAT THE PLACE WAS ONCE MUCH LESS WIDELY FREQUENTED...
1A
'THERE USED TO BE JUST A TINY TOWN THERE: HITCH CITY...'
'...DESERTED BY DAY...'
'...FAR TOO LIVELY BY NIGHT – OUTSIDE...'
CLOP!
'...OR INSIDE...'
CLOP!
CLOP!
'...TO THE POINT THAT MY FATHER, MAYOR OF THAT ILL-FATED PLACE, WAS FORCED TO CALL UPON LUCKY LUKE TO CLEAN UP THE TOWN...'
GOOD LUCK, LUKE.
GIVE ME THREE DAYS AND...
1B

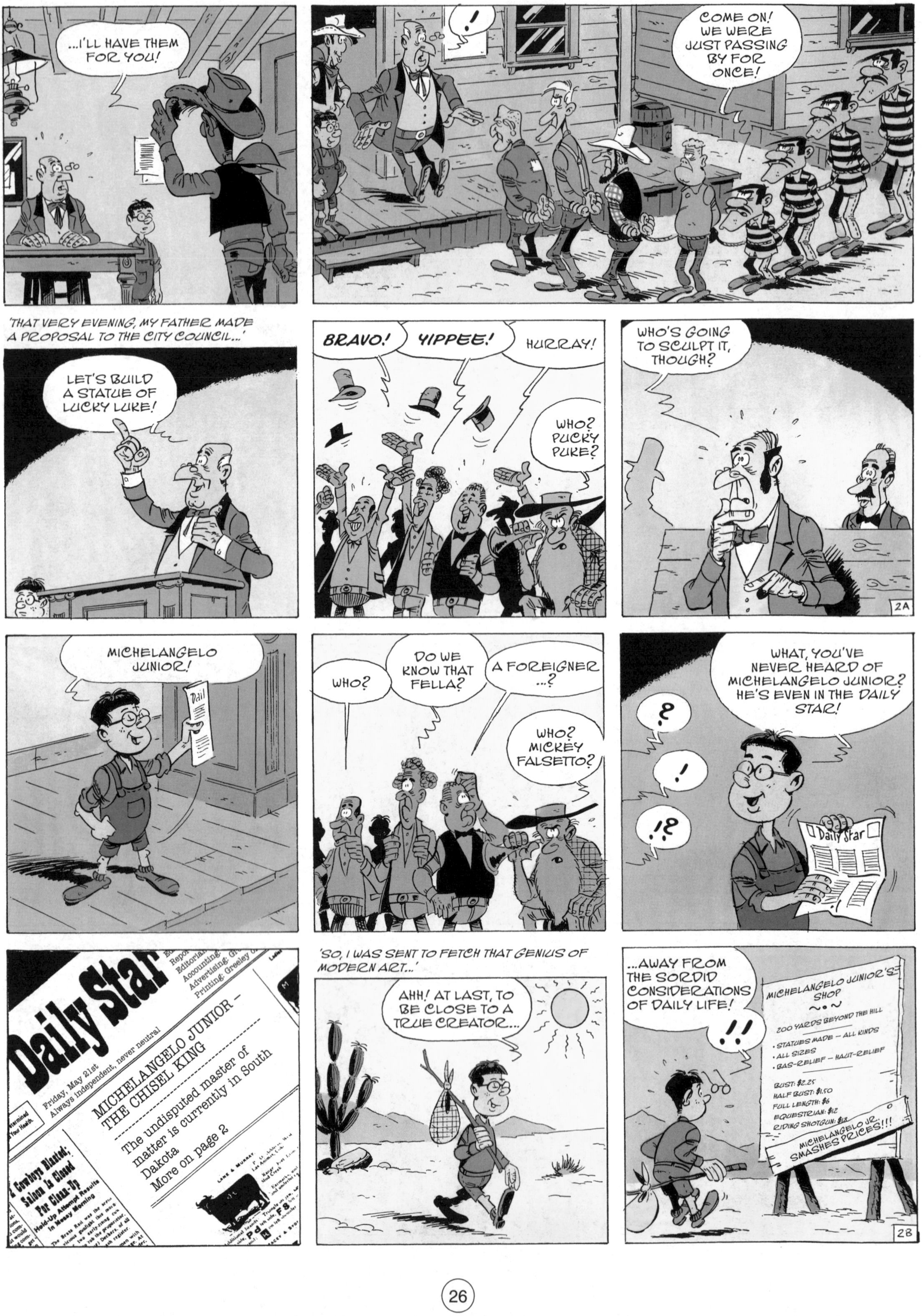

...I'LL HAVE THEM FOR YOU!
!
COME ON! WE WERE JUST PASSING BY FOR ONCE!
'THAT VERY EVENING, MY FATHER MADE A PROPOSAL TO THE CITY COUNCIL...'
LET'S BUILD A STATUE OF LUCKY LUKE!
BRAVO!
YIPPEE!
HURRAY!
WHO? PUCKY PUKE?
WHO'S GOING TO SCULPT IT, THOUGH?
2A
MICHELANGELO JUNIOR!
Dail
WHO?
DO WE KNOW THAT FELLA?
A FOREIGNER ...?
WHO? MICKEY FALSETTO?
WHAT, YOU'VE NEVER HEARD OF MICHELANGELO JUNIOR? HE'S EVEN IN THE DAILY STAR!
?
!
!?
Daily Star
Daily Star
Friday, May 21st
Always independent, never neutral
MICHELANGELO JUNIOR – THE CHISEL KING
The undisputed master of matter is currently in South Dakota
More on page 2
Cowboys Blasted; Saloon is Closed For Clean-Up
Hold-Up Attempt Results in Messy Morning
'SO, I WAS SENT TO FETCH THAT GENIUS OF MODERN ART...'
AHH! AT LAST, TO BE CLOSE TO A TRUE CREATOR...
...AWAY FROM THE SORDID CONSIDERATIONS OF DAILY LIFE!
!!
MICHELANGELO JUNIOR'S SHOP
200 YARDS BEYOND THE HILL
• STATUES MADE — ALL KINDS
• ALL SIZES
• BAS-RELIEF — HAUT-RELIEF
BUST: $2.25
HALF BUST: $1.50
FULL LENGTH: $6
EQUESTRIAN: $12
RIDING SHOTGUN: $18
MICHELANGELO JR. SMASHES PRICES!!!
2B

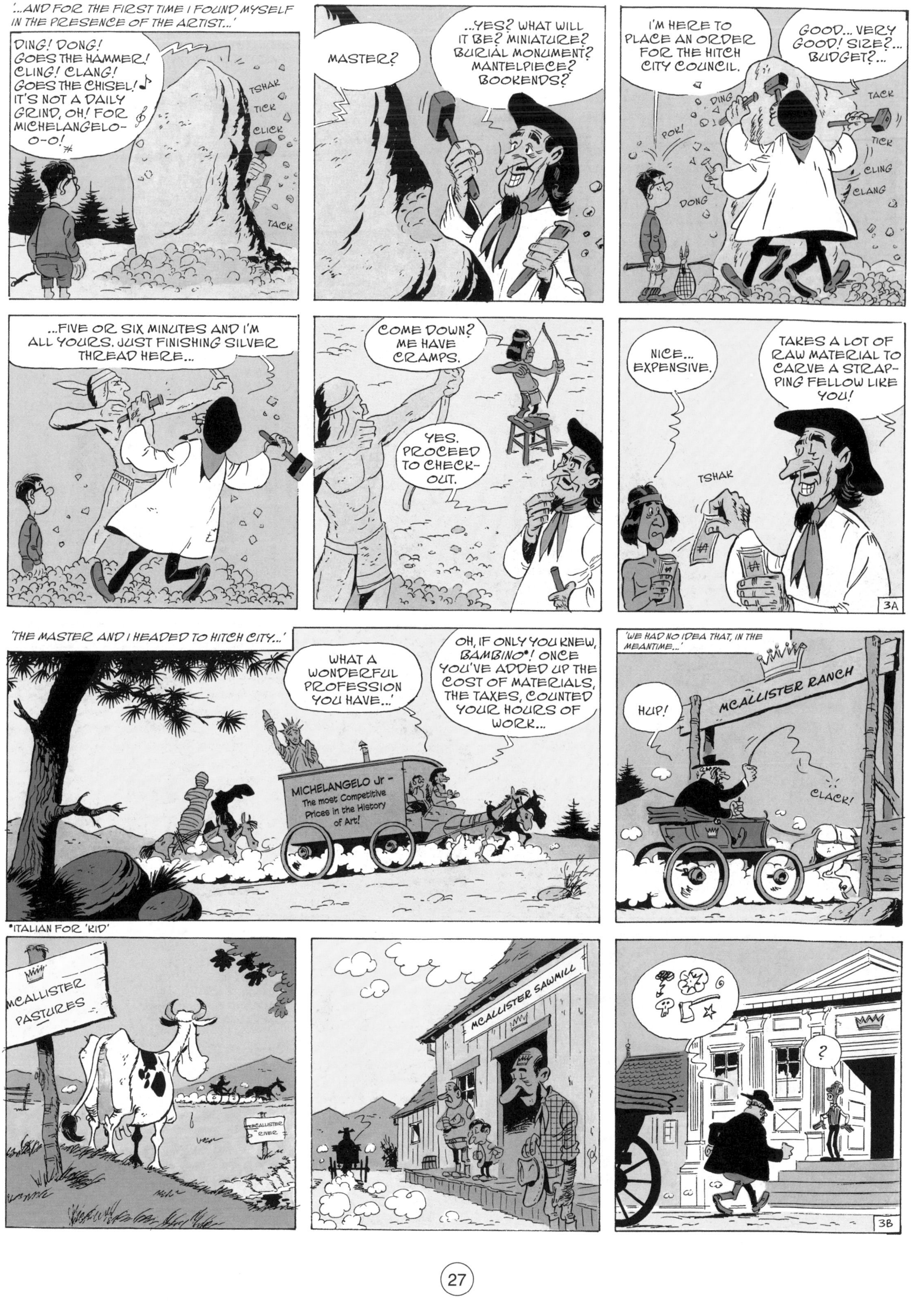
'...AND FOR THE FIRST TIME I FOUND MYSELF IN THE PRESENCE OF THE ARTIST...'
DING! DONG! GOES THE HAMMER! CLING! CLANG! GOES THE CHISEL! IT'S NOT A DAILY GRIND, OH! FOR MICHELANGELO-O-O!
TSHAK
TICK
CLICK
TACK
MASTER?
...YES? WHAT WILL IT BE? MINIATURE? BURIAL MONUMENT? MANTELPIECE? BOOKENDS?
I'M HERE TO PLACE AN ORDER FOR THE HITCH CITY COUNCIL.
GOOD... VERY GOOD! SIZE?... BUDGET?...
DING
POK!
TACK
TICK
CLING
CLANG
DONG
...FIVE OR SIX MINUTES AND I'M ALL YOURS. JUST FINISHING SILVER THREAD HERE...
COME DOWN? ME HAVE CRAMPS.
YES. PROCEED TO CHECK-OUT.
NICE... EXPENSIVE.
TAKES A LOT OF RAW MATERIAL TO CARVE A STRAPPING FELLOW LIKE YOU!
TSHAK
3A
'THE MASTER AND I HEADED TO HITCH CITY...'
WHAT A WONDERFUL PROFESSION YOU HAVE...'
OH, IF ONLY YOU KNEW, BAMBINO*! ONCE YOU'VE ADDED UP THE COST OF MATERIALS, THE TAXES, COUNTED YOUR HOURS OF WORK...
MICHELANGELO Jr - The most Competitive Prices in the History of Art!
'WE HAD NO IDEA THAT, IN THE MEANTIME...'
MCALLISTER RANCH
HUP!
CLACK!
*ITALIAN FOR 'KID'
MCALLISTER PASTURES
MCALLISTER RIVER
MCALLISTER SAWMILL
?
3B

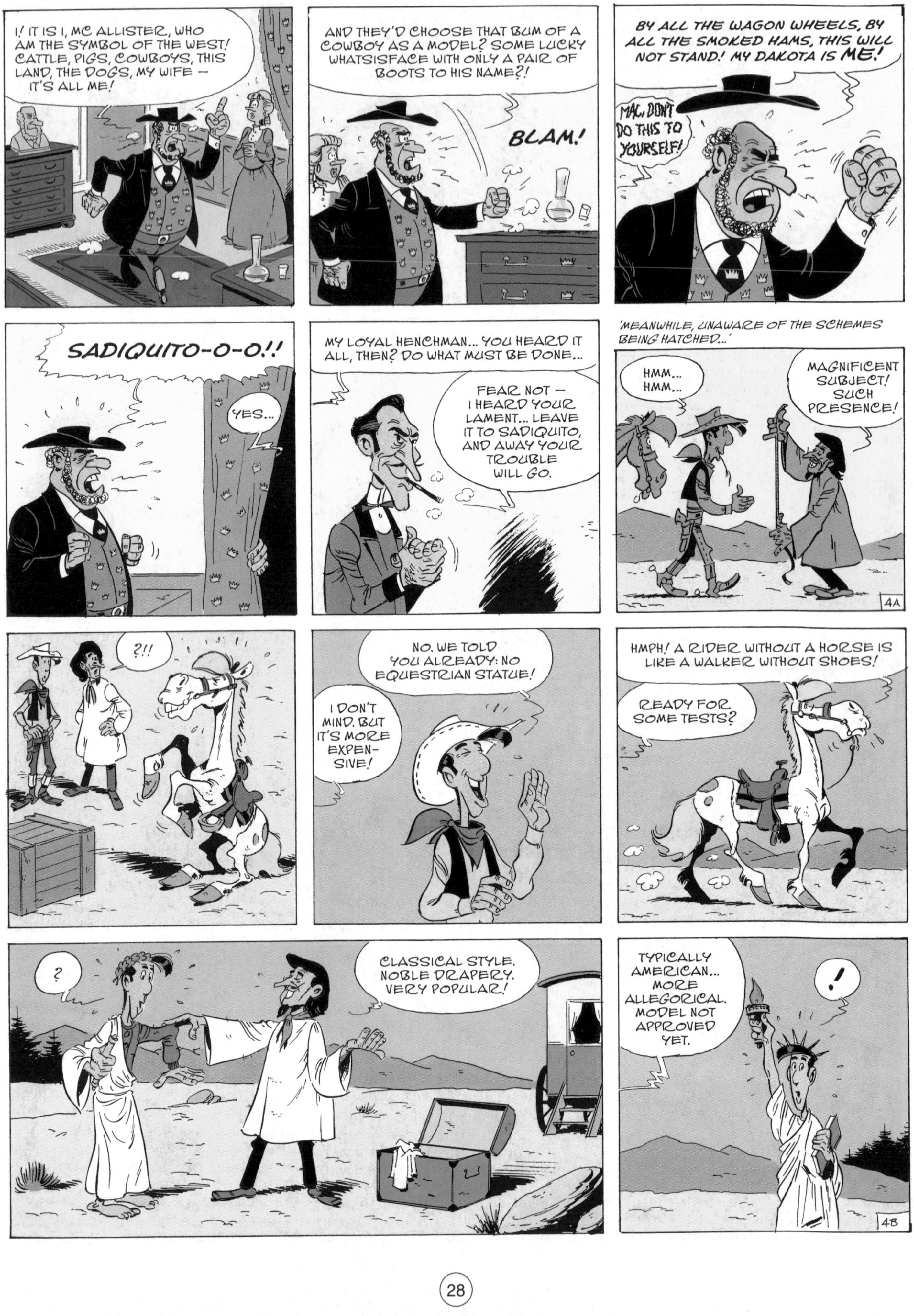
I! IT IS I, MC ALLISTER, WHO AM THE SYMBOL OF THE WEST! CATTLE, PIGS, COWBOYS, THIS LAND, THE DOGS, MY WIFE — IT'S ALL ME!
AND THEY'D CHOOSE THAT BUM OF A COWBOY AS A MODEL? SOME LUCKY WHATSISFACE WITH ONLY A PAIR OF BOOTS TO HIS NAME?!
BLAM!
BY ALL THE WAGON WHEELS, BY ALL THE SMOKED HAMS, THIS WILL NOT STAND! MY DAKOTA IS ME!
MAC, DON'T DO THIS TO YOURSELF!
SADIQUITO-O-O!!
YES...
MY LOYAL HENCHMAN... YOU HEARD IT ALL, THEN? DO WHAT MUST BE DONE...
FEAR NOT — I HEARD YOUR LAMENT... LEAVE IT TO SADIQUITO, AND AWAY YOUR TROUBLE WILL GO.
'MEANWHILE, UNAWARE OF THE SCHEMES BEING HATCHED...'
HMM... HMM...
MAGNIFICENT SUBJECT! SUCH PRESENCE!
4A
?!!
NO. WE TOLD YOU ALREADY: NO EQUESTRIAN STATUE!
I DON'T MIND. BUT IT'S MORE EXPEN-SIVE!
HMPH! A RIDER WITHOUT A HORSE IS LIKE A WALKER WITHOUT SHOES!
READY FOR SOME TESTS?
?
CLASSICAL STYLE. NOBLE DRAPERY. VERY POPULAR!
TYPICALLY AMERICAN... MORE ALLEGORICAL. MODEL NOT APPROVED YET.
!
4B

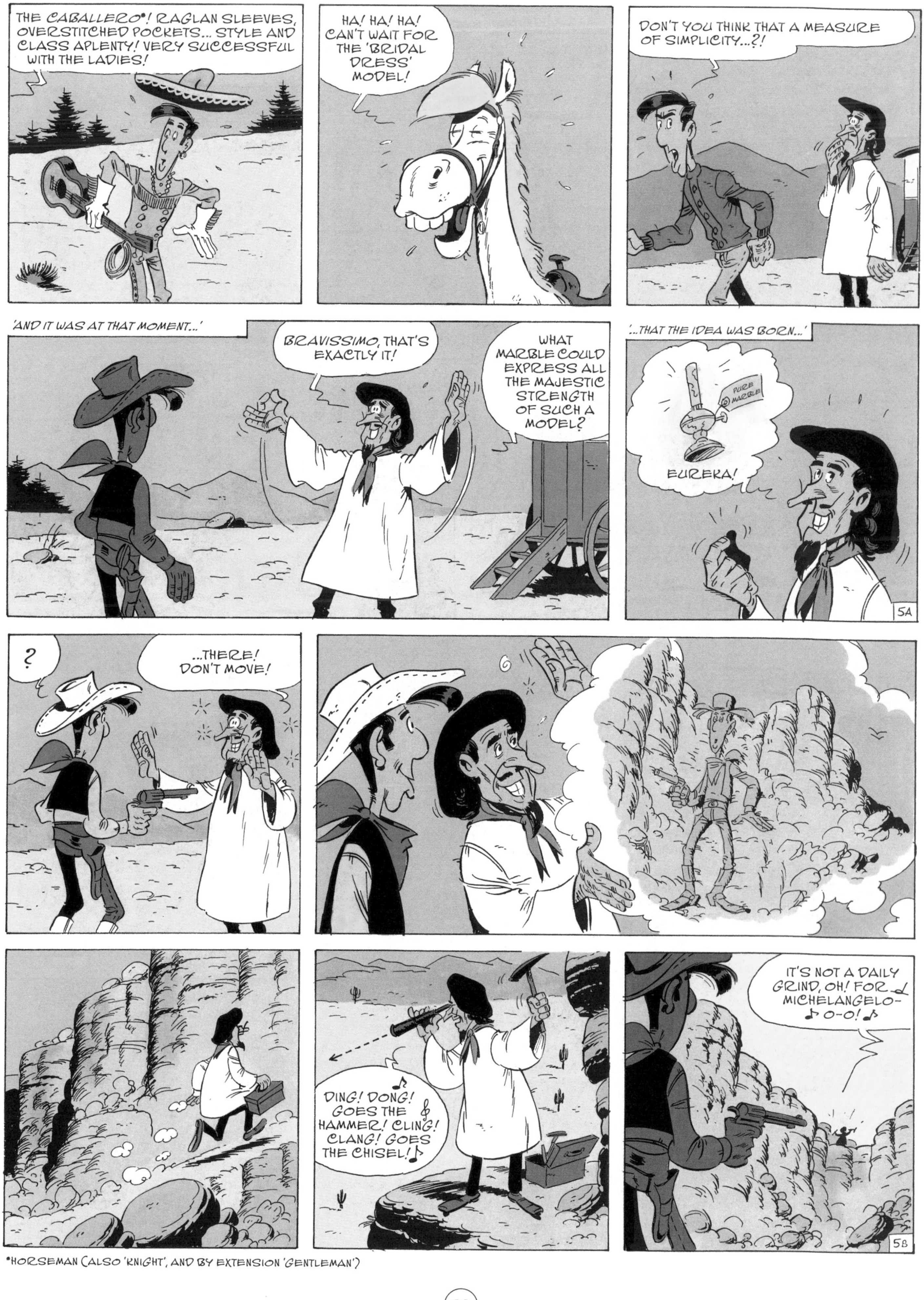
THE CABALLERO*! RAGLAN SLEEVES, OVERSTITCHED POCKETS... STYLE AND CLASS APLENTY! VERY SUCCESSFUL WITH THE LADIES!
HA! HA! HA! CAN'T WAIT FOR THE 'BRIDAL DRESS' MODEL!
DON'T YOU THINK THAT A MEASURE OF SIMPLICITY...?!
'AND IT WAS AT THAT MOMENT...'
BRAVISSIMO, THAT'S EXACTLY IT!
WHAT MARBLE COULD EXPRESS ALL THE MAJESTIC STRENGTH OF SUCH A MODEL?
'...THAT THE IDEA WAS BORN...'
PURE MARBLE
EUREKA!
5A
?
...THERE! DON'T MOVE!
DING! DONG! GOES THE HAMMER! CLING! CLANG! GOES THE CHISEL!
IT'S NOT A DAILY GRIND, OH! FOR MICHELANGELO-O-O!
5B

*HORSEMAN (ALSO 'KNIGHT', AND BY EXTENSION 'GENTLEMAN')

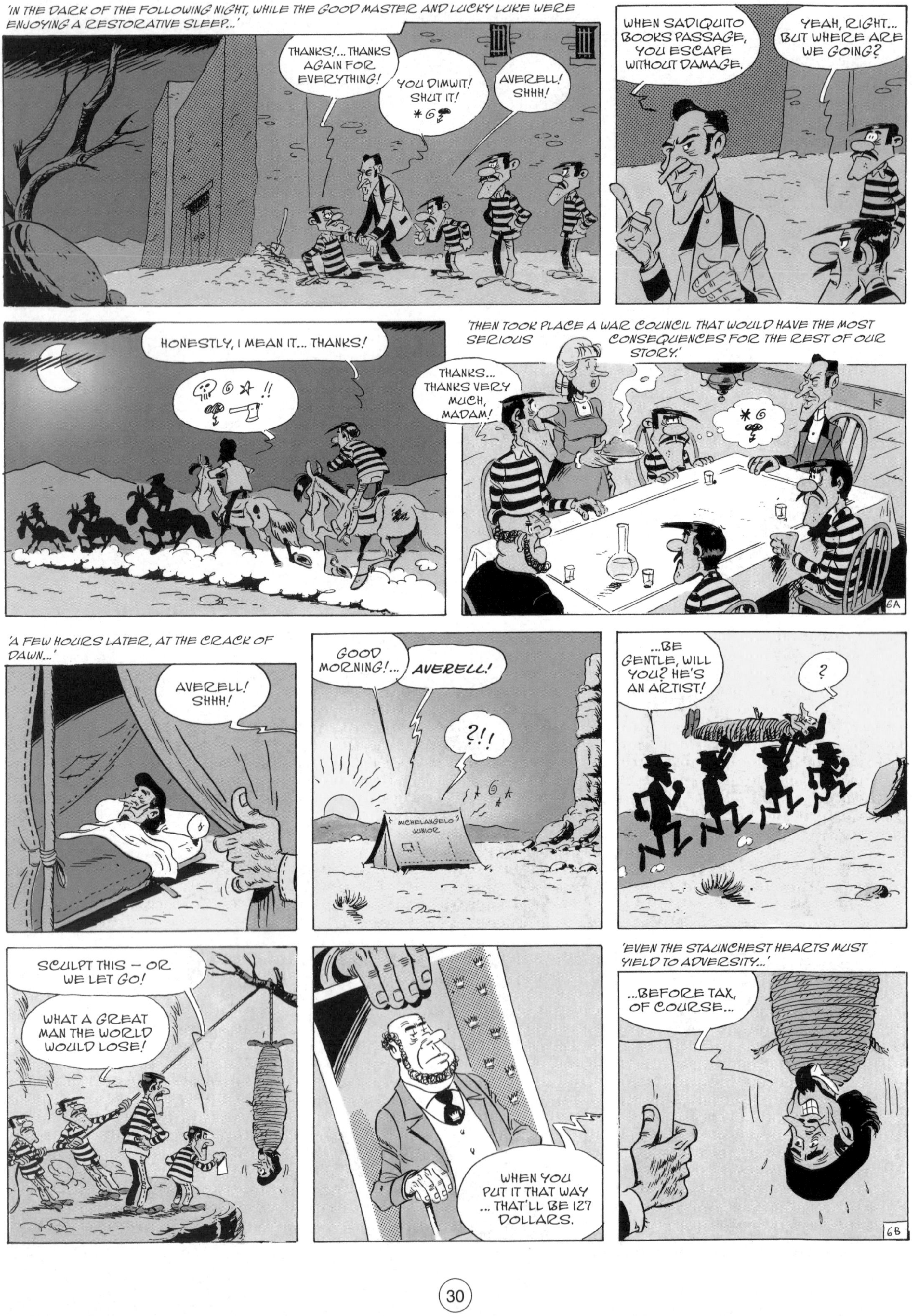
'IN THE DARK OF THE FOLLOWING NIGHT, WHILE THE GOOD MASTER AND LUCKY LUKE WERE ENJOYING A RESTORATIVE SLEEP...'
THANKS!... THANKS AGAIN FOR EVERYTHING!
YOU DIMWIT! SHUT IT!
AVERELL! SHHH!
WHEN SADIQUITO BOOKS PASSAGE, YOU ESCAPE WITHOUT DAMAGE.
YEAH, RIGHT... BUT WHERE ARE WE GOING?
HONESTLY, I MEAN IT... THANKS!
'THEN TOOK PLACE A WAR COUNCIL THAT WOULD HAVE THE MOST SERIOUS CONSEQUENCES FOR THE REST OF OUR STORY.'
THANKS... THANKS VERY MUCH, MADAM!
6A
'A FEW HOURS LATER, AT THE CRACK OF DAWN...'
AVERELL! SHHH!
GOOD MORNING!...
AVERELL!
?!!
MICHELANGELO JUNIOR
...BE GENTLE, WILL YOU? HE'S AN ARTIST!
?
SCULPT THIS – OR WE LET GO!
WHAT A GREAT MAN THE WORLD WOULD LOSE!
WHEN YOU PUT IT THAT WAY ... THAT'LL BE 127 DOLLARS.
'EVEN THE STAUNCHEST HEARTS MUST YIELD TO ADVERSITY...'
...BEFORE TAX, OF COURSE...
6B

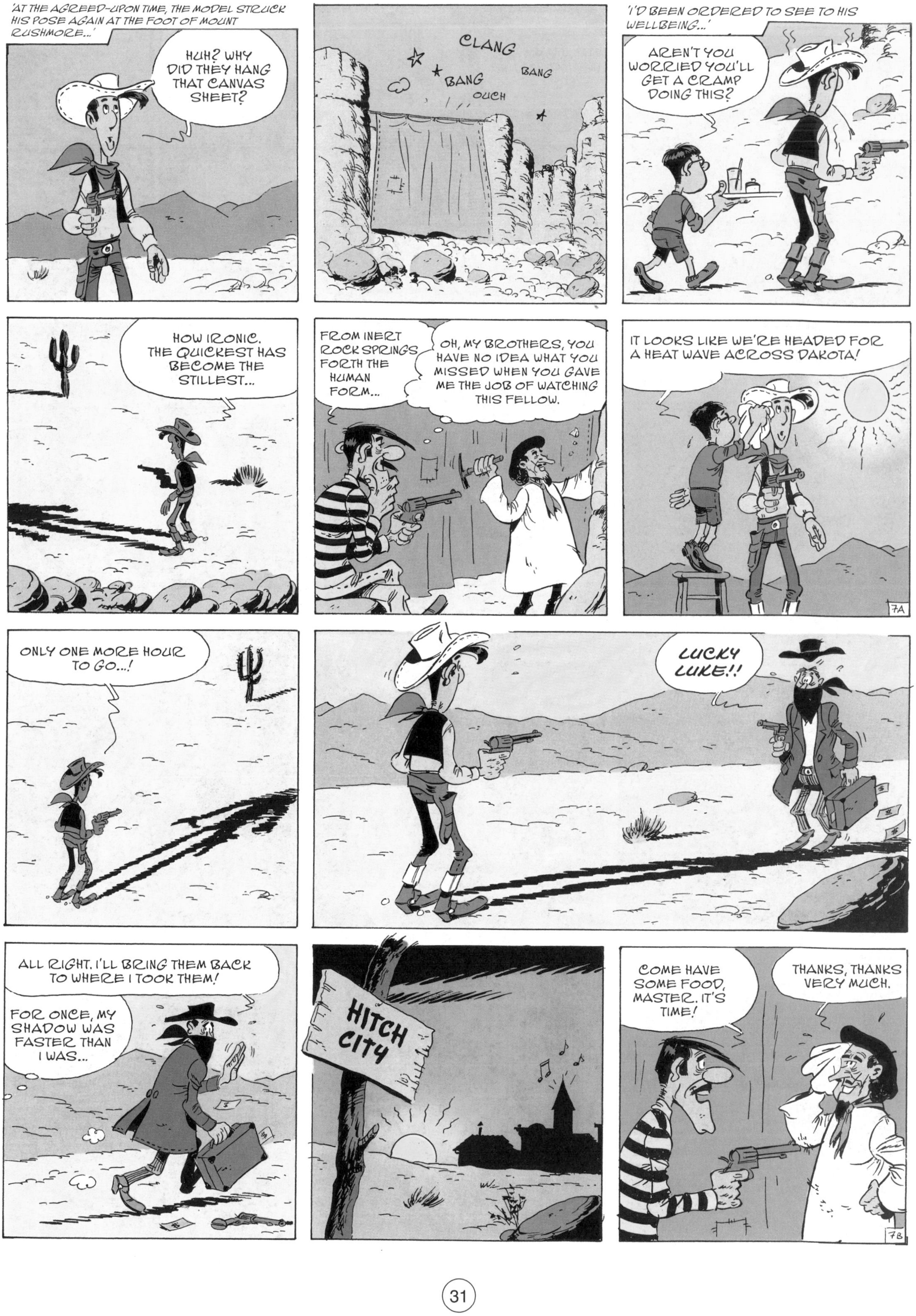
'AT THE AGREED-UPON TIME, THE MODEL STRUCK HIS POSE AGAIN AT THE FOOT OF MOUNT RUSHMORE...'
HUH? WHY DID THEY HANG THAT CANVAS SHEET?
CLANG
BANG
BANG
OUCH
'I'D BEEN ORDERED TO SEE TO HIS WELLBEING...'
AREN'T YOU WORRIED YOU'LL GET A CRAMP DOING THIS?
HOW IRONIC. THE QUICKEST HAS BECOME THE STILLEST...
FROM INERT ROCK SPRINGS FORTH THE HUMAN FORM...
OH, MY BROTHERS, YOU HAVE NO IDEA WHAT YOU MISSED WHEN YOU GAVE ME THE JOB OF WATCHING THIS FELLOW.
IT LOOKS LIKE WE'RE HEADED FOR A HEAT WAVE ACROSS DAKOTA!
7A
ONLY ONE MORE HOUR TO GO...!
LUCKY LUKE!!
ALL RIGHT. I'LL BRING THEM BACK TO WHERE I TOOK THEM!
FOR ONCE, MY SHADOW WAS FASTER THAN I WAS...
HITCH CITY
COME HAVE SOME FOOD, MASTER. IT'S TIME!
THANKS, THANKS VERY MUCH.
7B

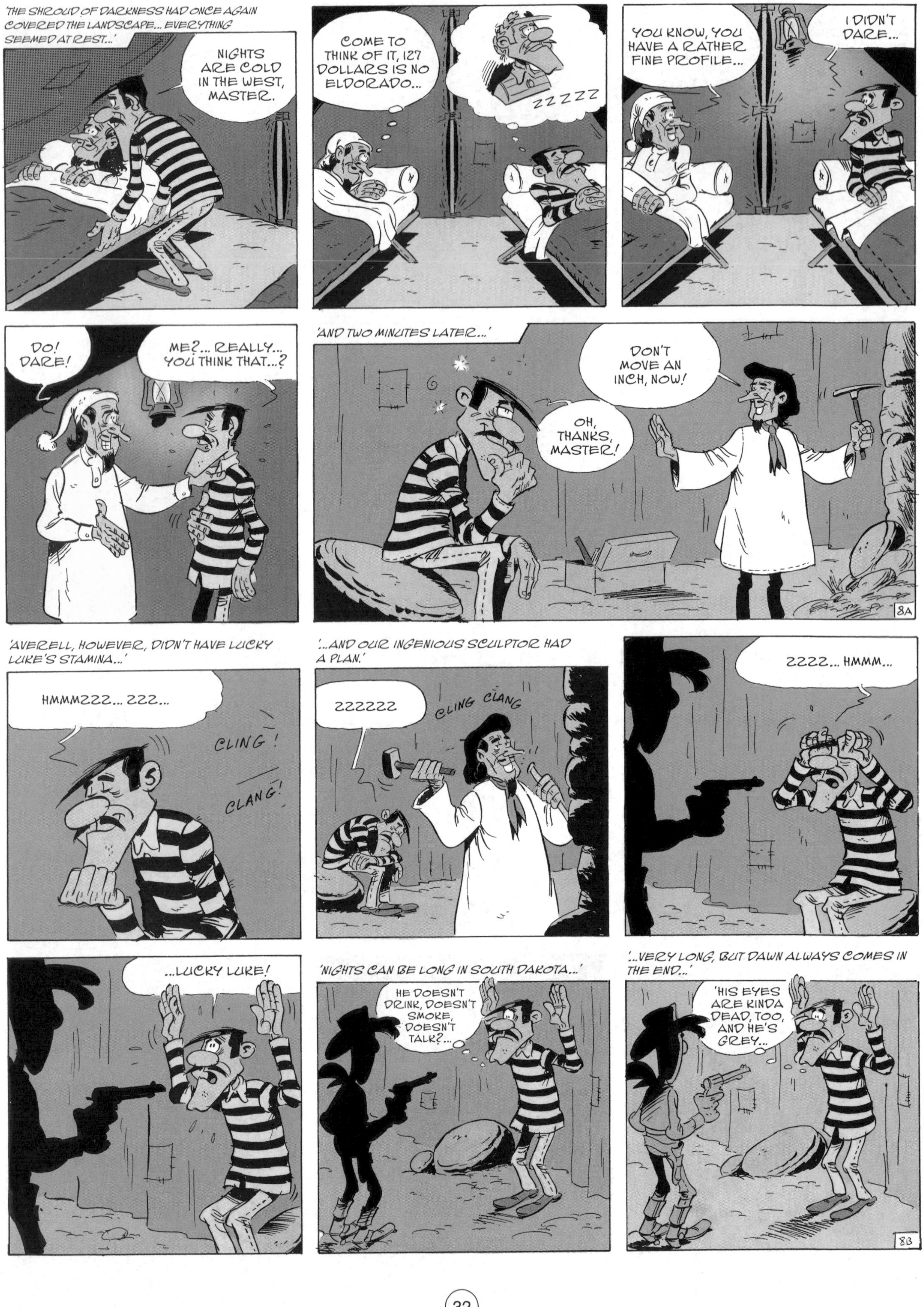
'THE SHROUD OF DARKNESS HAD ONCE AGAIN COVERED THE LANDSCAPE... EVERYTHING SEEMED AT REST...'
NIGHTS ARE COLD IN THE WEST, MASTER.
COME TO THINK OF IT, 127 DOLLARS IS NO ELDORADO...
ZZZZZ
YOU KNOW, YOU HAVE A RATHER FINE PROFILE...
I DIDN'T DARE...
DO! DARE!
ME?... REALLY... YOU THINK THAT...?
'AND TWO MINUTES LATER...'
DON'T MOVE AN INCH, NOW!
OH, THANKS, MASTER!
8A
'AVERELL, HOWEVER, DIDN'T HAVE LUCKY LUKE'S STAMINA...'
HMMMZZZ... ZZZ...
CLING!
CLANG!
'...AND OUR INGENIOUS SCULPTOR HAD A PLAN.'
ZZZZZZ
CLING CLANG
ZZZZ... HMMM...
...LUCKY LUKE!
'NIGHTS CAN BE LONG IN SOUTH DAKOTA...'
HE DOESN'T DRINK, DOESN'T SMOKE, DOESN'T TALK?...
'...VERY LONG, BUT DAWN ALWAYS COMES IN THE END...'
'HIS EYES ARE KINDA DEAD, TOO, AND HE'S GREY...
8B

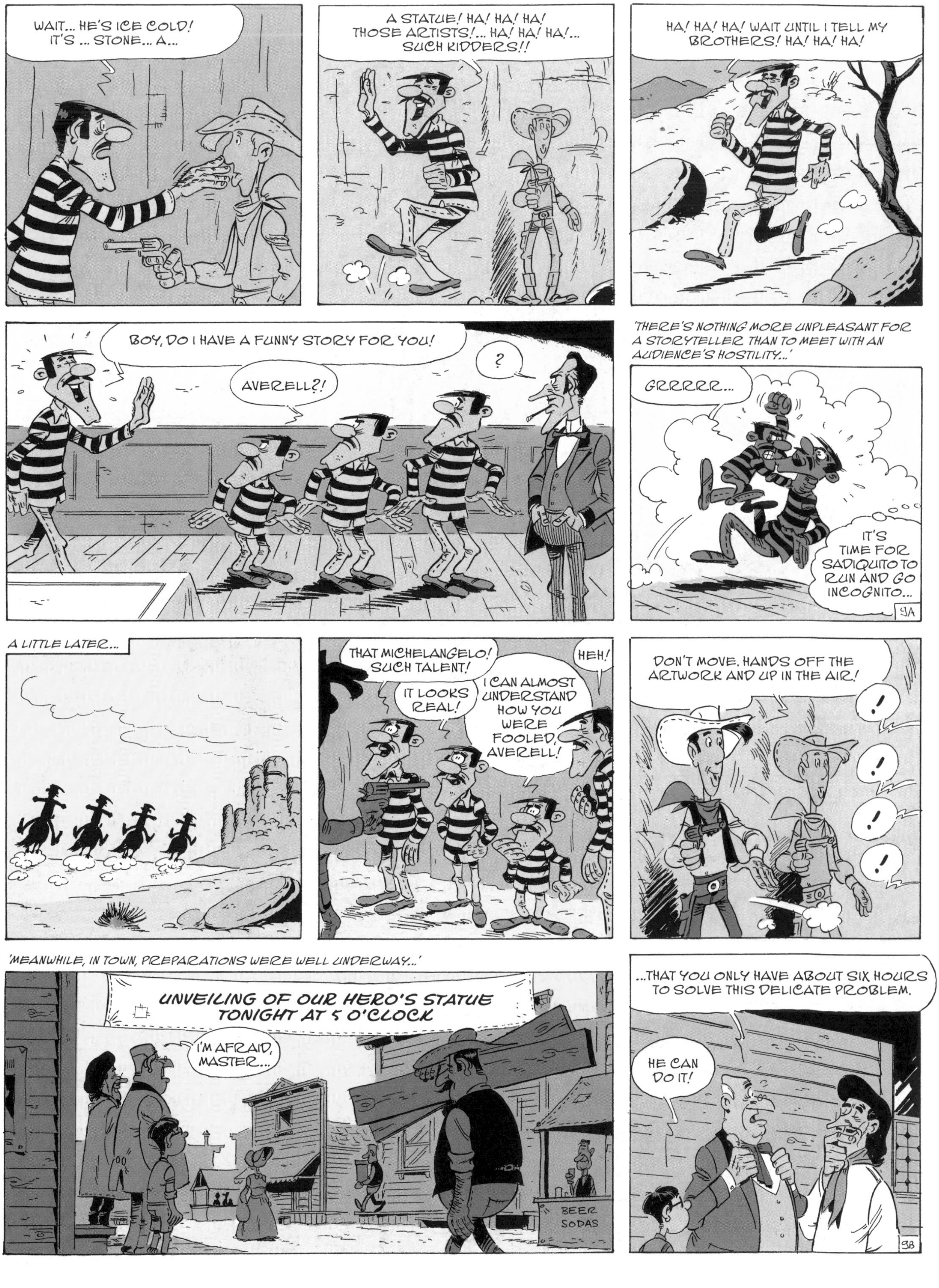
WAIT... HE'S ICE COLD! IT'S ... STONE... A...
A STATUE! HA! HA! HA! THOSE ARTISTS!... HA! HA! HA!... SUCH KIDDERS!!
HA! HA! HA! WAIT UNTIL I TELL MY BROTHERS! HA! HA! HA!
BOY, DO I HAVE A FUNNY STORY FOR YOU!
AVERELL?!
?
'THERE'S NOTHING MORE UNPLEASANT FOR A STORYTELLER THAN TO MEET WITH AN AUDIENCE'S HOSTILITY...'
GRRRRR...
IT'S TIME FOR SADIQUITO TO RUN AND GO INCOGNITO...
A LITTLE LATER...
THAT MICHELANGELO! SUCH TALENT!
IT LOOKS REAL!
HEH!
I CAN ALMOST UNDERSTAND HOW YOU WERE FOOLED, AVERELL!
DON'T MOVE. HANDS OFF THE ARTWORK AND UP IN THE AIR!
!
!
!
!
'MEANWHILE, IN TOWN, PREPARATIONS WERE WELL UNDERWAY...'
UNVEILING OF OUR HERO'S STATUE TONIGHT AT 5 O'CLOCK
I'M AFRAID, MASTER...
BEER SODAS
...THAT YOU ONLY HAVE ABOUT SIX HOURS TO SOLVE THIS DELICATE PROBLEM.
HE CAN DO IT!

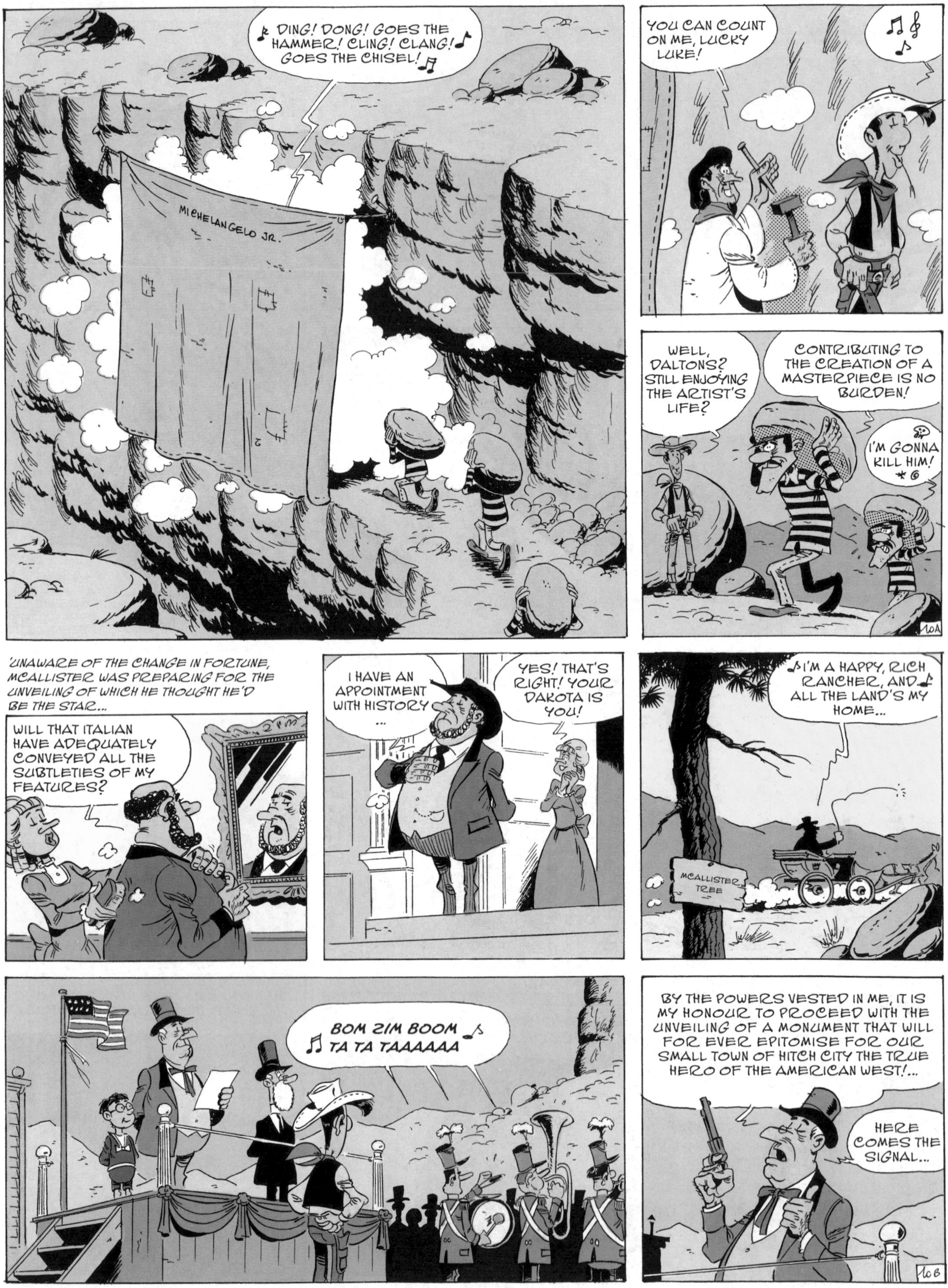

DING! DONG! GOES THE HAMMER! CLING! CLANG! GOES THE CHISEL!
MICHELANGELO JR.
YOU CAN COUNT ON ME, LUCKY LUKE!
WELL, DALTONS? STILL ENJOYING THE ARTIST'S LIFE?
CONTRIBUTING TO THE CREATION OF A MASTERPIECE IS NO BURDEN!
I'M GONNA KILL HIM!
UNAWARE OF THE CHANGE IN FORTUNE, MCALLISTER WAS PREPARING FOR THE UNVEILING OF WHICH HE THOUGHT HE'D BE THE STAR...
WILL THAT ITALIAN HAVE ADEQUATELY CONVEYED ALL THE SUBTLETIES OF MY FEATURES?
I HAVE AN APPOINTMENT WITH HISTORY ...
YES! THAT'S RIGHT! YOUR DAKOTA IS YOU!
I'M A HAPPY, RICH RANCHER, AND ALL THE LAND'S MY HOME...
MCALLISTER TREE
BOM ZIM BOOM TA TA TAAAAAA
BY THE POWERS VESTED IN ME, IT IS MY HONOUR TO PROCEED WITH THE UNVEILING OF A MONUMENT THAT WILL FOR EVER EPITOMISE FOR OUR SMALL TOWN OF HITCH CITY THE TRUE HERO OF THE AMERICAN WEST!...
HERE COMES THE SIGNAL...

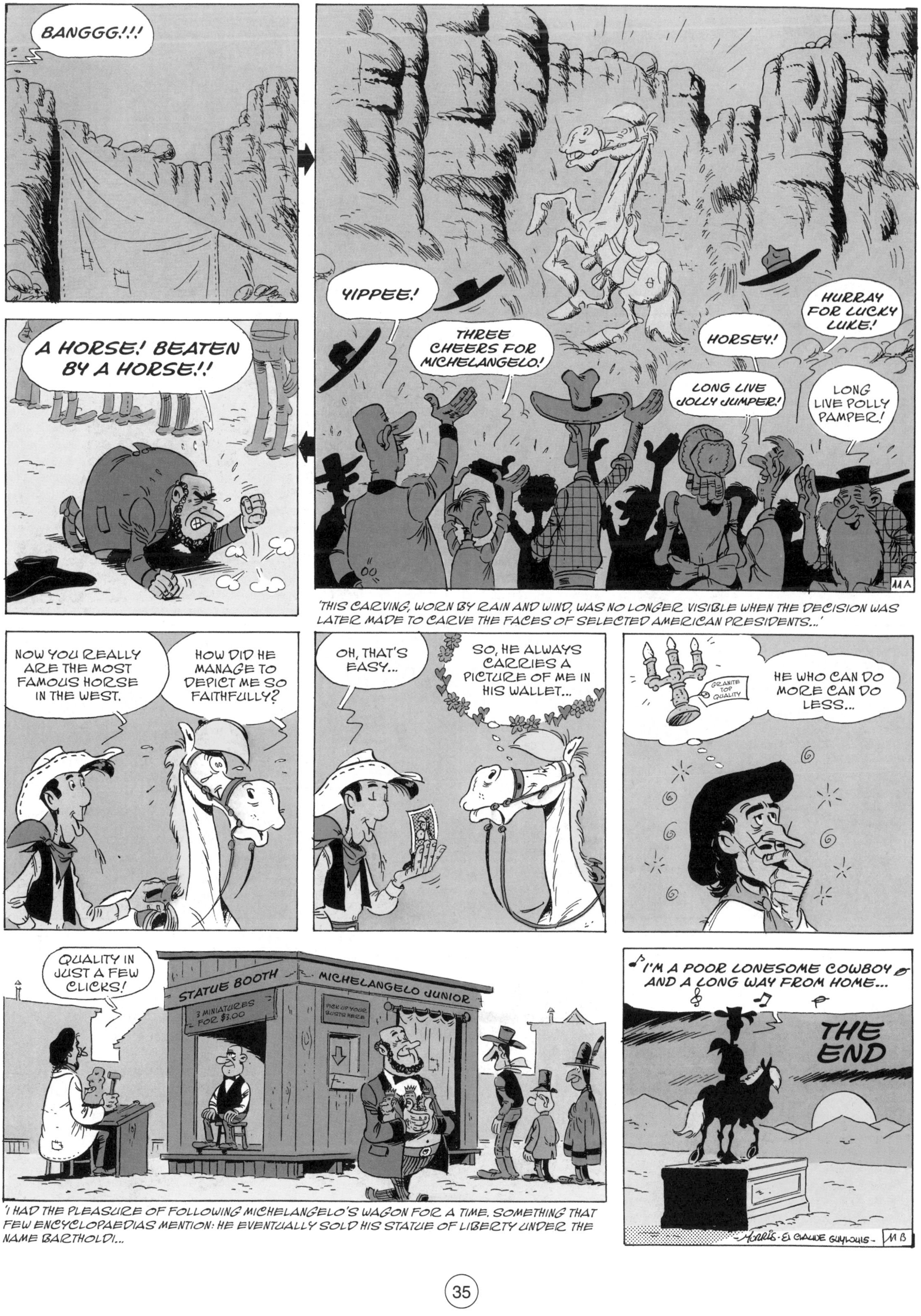
BANGGG!!!
YIPPEE!
THREE CHEERS FOR MICHELANGELO!
HORSEY!
HURRAY FOR LUCKY LUKE!
LONG LIVE JOLLY JUMPER!
LONG LIVE POLLY PAMPER!
A HORSE! BEATEN BY A HORSE!!
'THIS CARVING, WORN BY RAIN AND WIND, WAS NO LONGER VISIBLE WHEN THE DECISION WAS LATER MADE TO CARVE THE FACES OF SELECTED AMERICAN PRESIDENTS...'
NOW YOU REALLY ARE THE MOST FAMOUS HORSE IN THE WEST.
HOW DID HE MANAGE TO DEPICT ME SO FAITHFULLY?
OH, THAT'S EASY...
SO, HE ALWAYS CARRIES A PICTURE OF ME IN HIS WALLET...
GRANITE TOP QUALITY
HE WHO CAN DO MORE CAN DO LESS...
QUALITY IN JUST A FEW CLICKS!
STATUE BOOTH
MICHELANGELO JUNIOR
3 MINIATURES FOR $3.00
PICK UP YOUR BUSTS HERE
'I HAD THE PLEASURE OF FOLLOWING MICHELANGELO'S WAGON FOR A TIME. SOMETHING THAT FEW ENCYCLOPAEDIAS MENTION: HE EVENTUALLY SOLD HIS STATUE OF LIBERTY UNDER THE NAME BARTHOLDI...
I'M A POOR LONESOME COWBOY AND A LONG WAY FROM HOME...
THE END

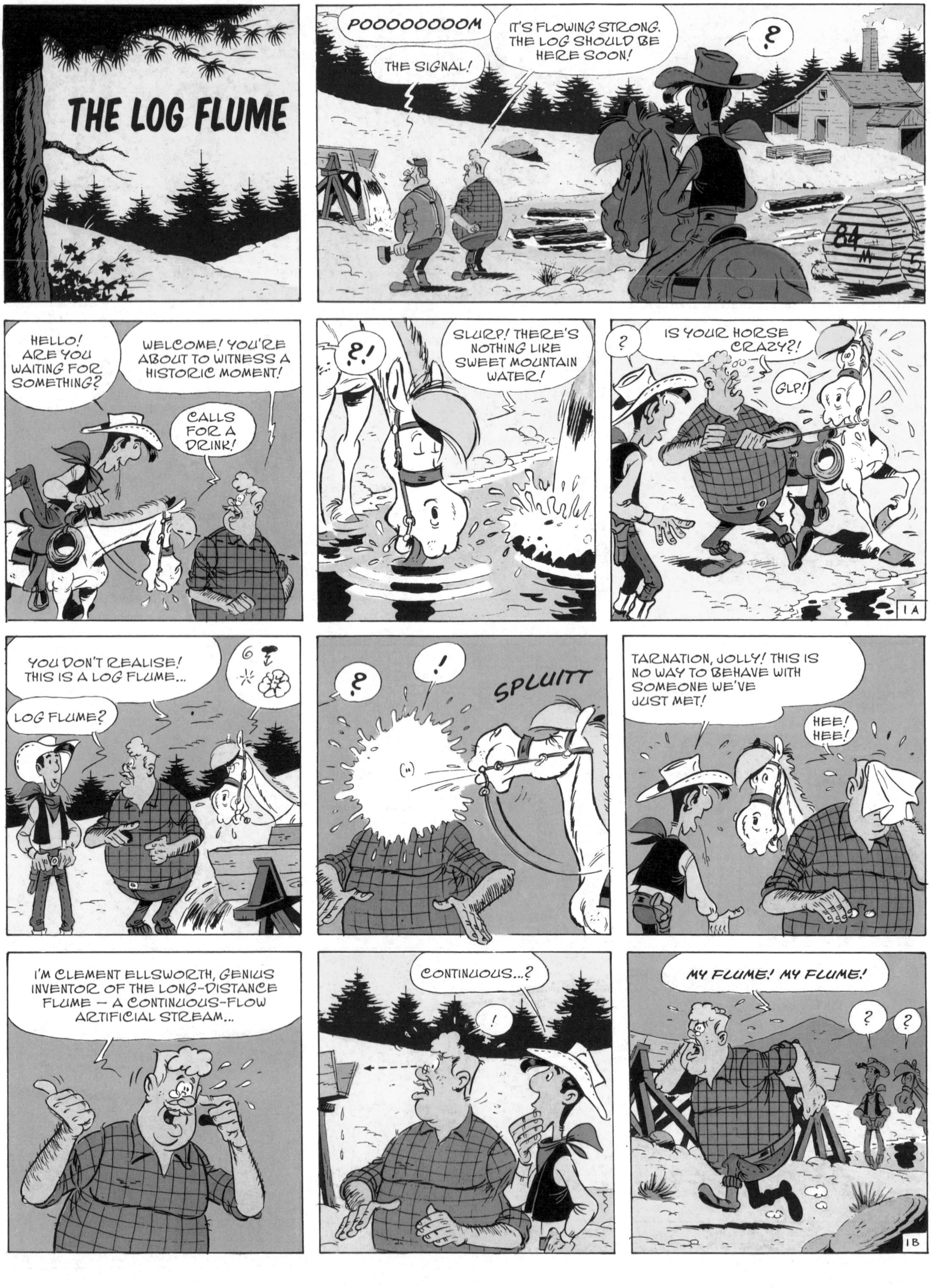
THE LOG FLUME
POOOOOOOOM
THE SIGNAL!
IT'S FLOWING STRONG. THE LOG SHOULD BE HERE SOON!
?
HELLO! ARE YOU WAITING FOR SOMETHING?
WELCOME! YOU'RE ABOUT TO WITNESS A HISTORIC MOMENT!
CALLS FOR A DRINK!
?!
SLURP! THERE'S NOTHING LIKE SWEET MOUNTAIN WATER!
?
IS YOUR HORSE CRAZY?!
GLP!
1A
YOU DON'T REALISE! THIS IS A LOG FLUME...
LOG FLUME?
?
!
SPLUITT
TARNATION, JOLLY! THIS IS NO WAY TO BEHAVE WITH SOMEONE WE'VE JUST MET!
HEE! HEE!
I'M CLEMENT ELLSWORTH, GENIUS INVENTOR OF THE LONG-DISTANCE FLUME – A CONTINUOUS-FLOW ARTIFICIAL STREAM...
CONTINUOUS...?
!
MY FLUME! MY FLUME!
?
?
1B

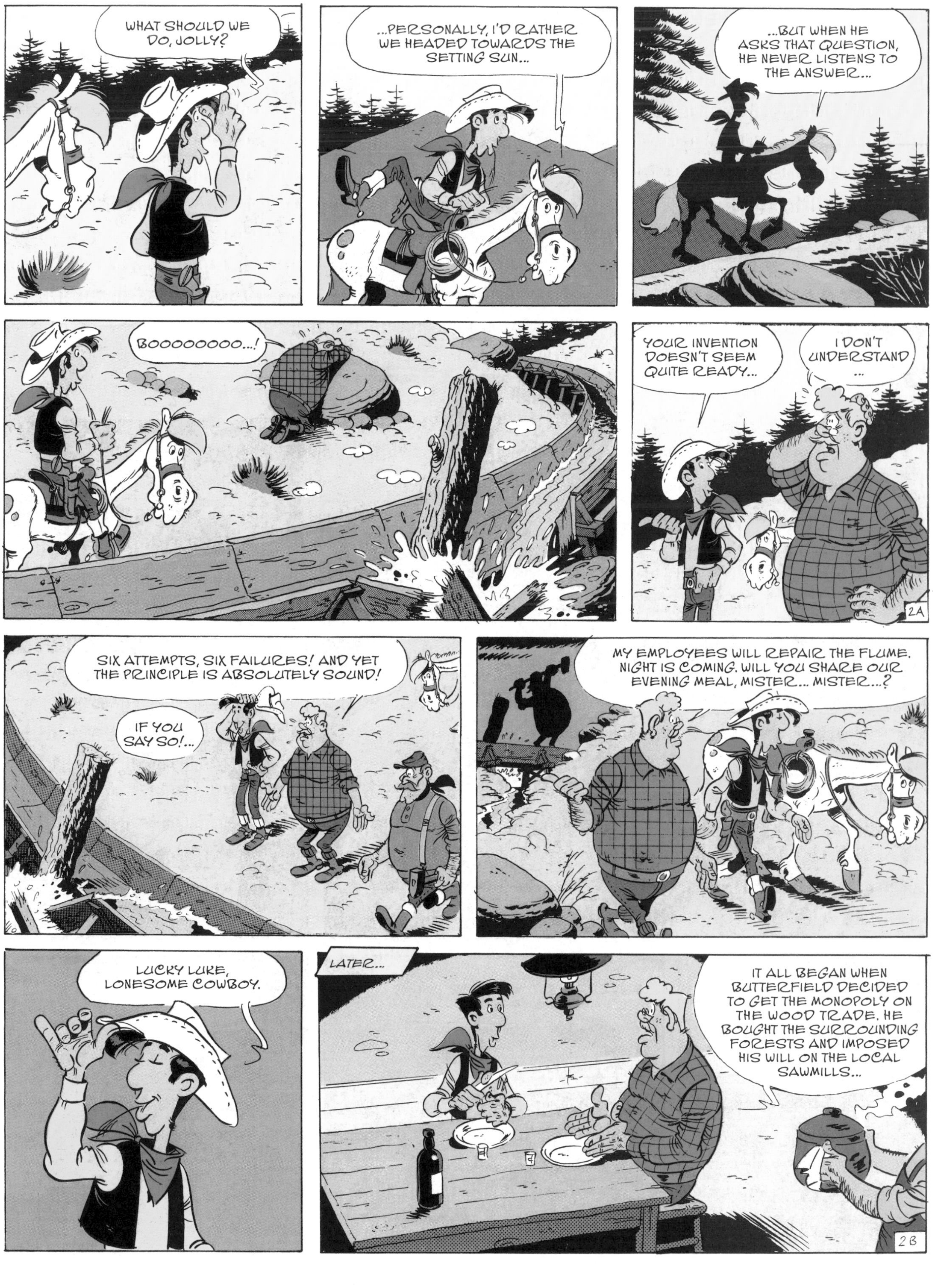
WHAT SHOULD WE DO, JOLLY?
...PERSONALLY, I'D RATHER WE HEADED TOWARDS THE SETTING SUN...
...BUT WHEN HE ASKS THAT QUESTION, HE NEVER LISTENS TO THE ANSWER...
BOOOOOOOOO...!
YOUR INVENTION DOESN'T SEEM QUITE READY...
I DON'T UNDERSTAND ...
2A
SIX ATTEMPTS, SIX FAILURES! AND YET THE PRINCIPLE IS ABSOLUTELY SOUND!
IF YOU SAY SO!...
MY EMPLOYEES WILL REPAIR THE FLUME. NIGHT IS COMING. WILL YOU SHARE OUR EVENING MEAL, MISTER... MISTER...?
LUCKY LUKE, LONESOME COWBOY.
LATER...
IT ALL BEGAN WHEN BUTTERFIELD DECIDED TO GET THE MONOPOLY ON THE WOOD TRADE. HE BOUGHT THE SURROUNDING FORESTS AND IMPOSED HIS WILL ON THE LOCAL SAWMILLS...
2B

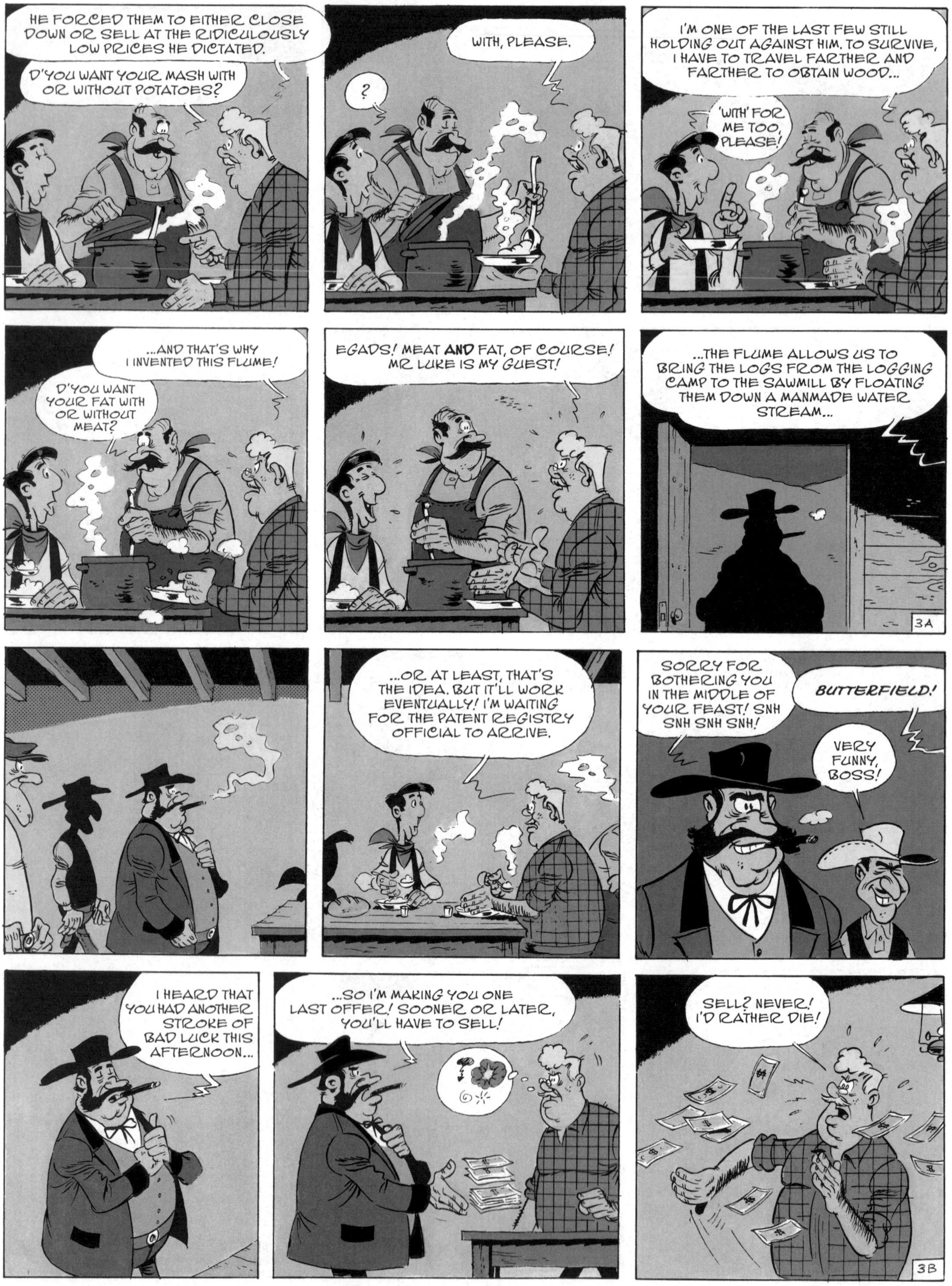
HE FORCED THEM TO EITHER CLOSE DOWN OR SELL AT THE RIDICULOUSLY LOW PRICES HE DICTATED.
D'YOU WANT YOUR MASH WITH OR WITHOUT POTATOES?
WITH, PLEASE.
?
I'M ONE OF THE LAST FEW STILL HOLDING OUT AGAINST HIM. TO SURVIVE, I HAVE TO TRAVEL FARTHER AND FARTHER TO OBTAIN WOOD...
'WITH' FOR ME TOO, PLEASE!
...AND THAT'S WHY I INVENTED THIS FLUME!
D'YOU WANT YOUR FAT WITH OR WITHOUT MEAT?
EGADS! MEAT AND FAT, OF COURSE! MR LUKE IS MY GUEST!
...THE FLUME ALLOWS US TO BRING THE LOGS FROM THE LOGGING CAMP TO THE SAWMILL BY FLOATING THEM DOWN A MANMADE WATER STREAM...
3A
...OR AT LEAST, THAT'S THE IDEA. BUT IT'LL WORK EVENTUALLY! I'M WAITING FOR THE PATENT REGISTRY OFFICIAL TO ARRIVE.
SORRY FOR BOTHERING YOU IN THE MIDDLE OF YOUR FEAST! SNH SNH SNH SNH!
BUTTERFIELD!
VERY FUNNY, BOSS!
I HEARD THAT YOU HAD ANOTHER STROKE OF BAD LUCK THIS AFTERNOON...
...SO I'M MAKING YOU ONE LAST OFFER! SOONER OR LATER, YOU'LL HAVE TO SELL!
SELL? NEVER! I'D RATHER DIE!
3B

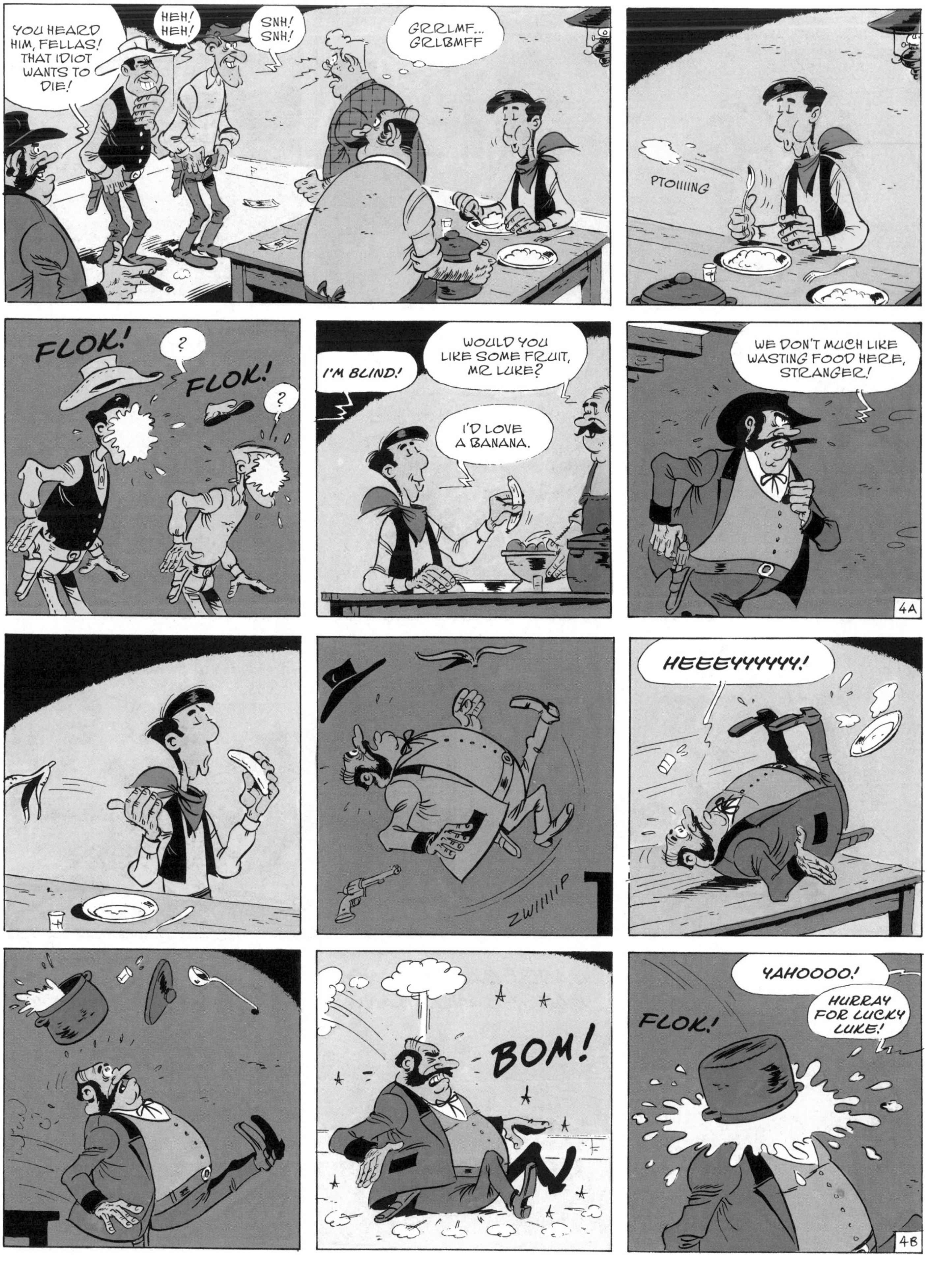
YOU HEARD HIM, FELLAS! THAT IDIOT WANTS TO DIE!
HEH! HEH!
SNH! SNH!
GRRLMF... GRLBMFF
PTOIIIING
FLOK!
?
FLOK!
?
I'M BLIND!
WOULD YOU LIKE SOME FRUIT, MR LUKE?
I'D LOVE A BANANA.
WE DON'T MUCH LIKE WASTING FOOD HERE, STRANGER!
4A
ZWIIIIIP
HEEEYYYYY!
BOM!
FLOK!
YAHOOOO!
HURRAY FOR LUCKY LUKE!
4B

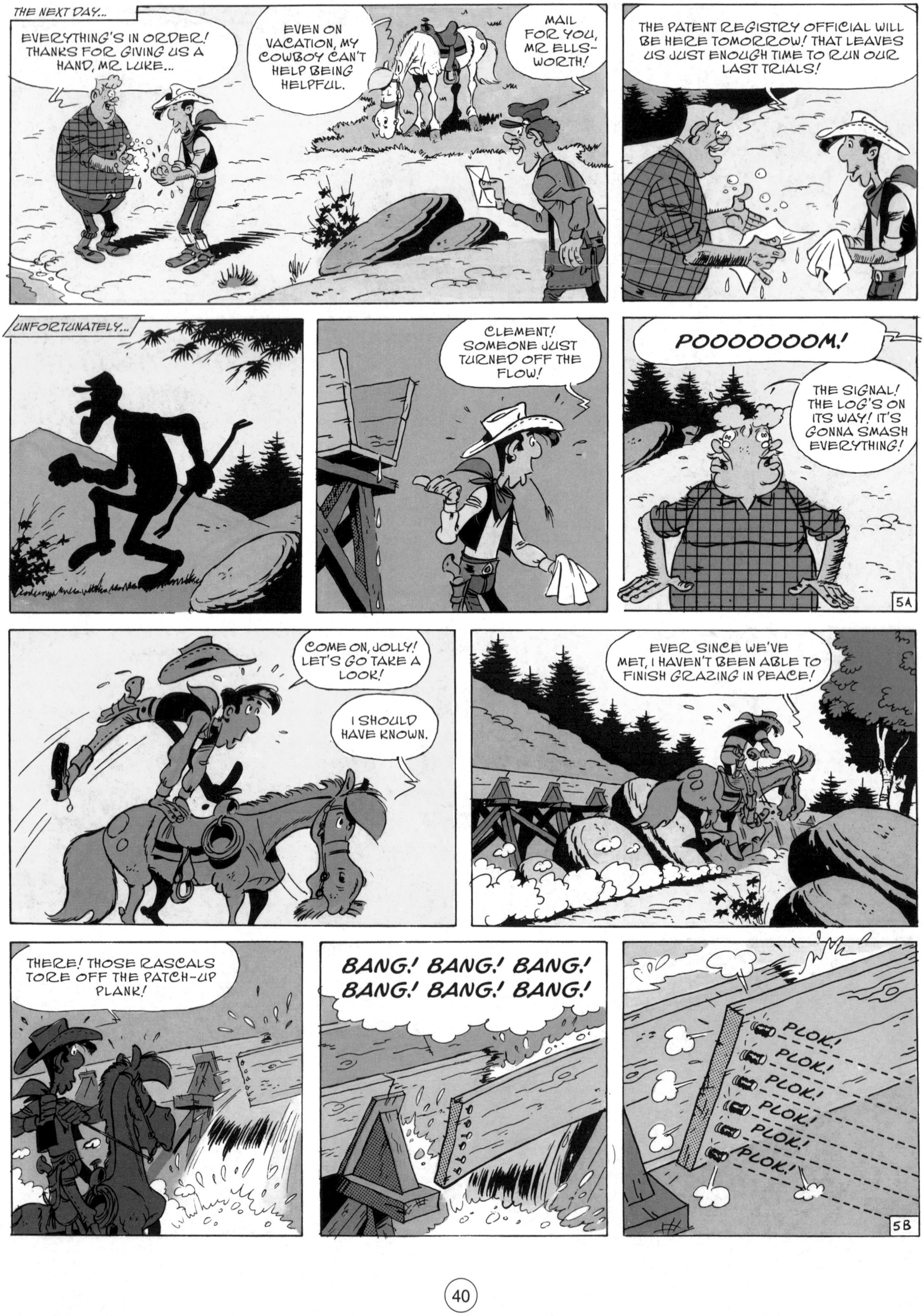
THE NEXT DAY...
EVERYTHING'S IN ORDER! THANKS FOR GIVING US A HAND, MR LUKE...
EVEN ON VACATION, MY COWBOY CAN'T HELP BEING HELPFUL.
MAIL FOR YOU, MR ELLSWORTH!
THE PATENT REGISTRY OFFICIAL WILL BE HERE TOMORROW! THAT LEAVES US JUST ENOUGH TIME TO RUN OUR LAST TRIALS!
UNFORTUNATELY...
CLEMENT! SOMEONE JUST TURNED OFF THE FLOW!
POOOOOOOM!
THE SIGNAL! THE LOG'S ON ITS WAY! IT'S GONNA SMASH EVERYTHING!
5A
COME ON, JOLLY! LET'S GO TAKE A LOOK!
I SHOULD HAVE KNOWN.
EVER SINCE WE'VE MET, I HAVEN'T BEEN ABLE TO FINISH GRAZING IN PEACE!
THERE! THOSE RASCALS TORE OFF THE PATCH-UP PLANK!
BANG! BANG! BANG! BANG! BANG! BANG!
PLOK!
PLOK!
PLOK!
PLOK!
PLOK!
PLOK!
5B

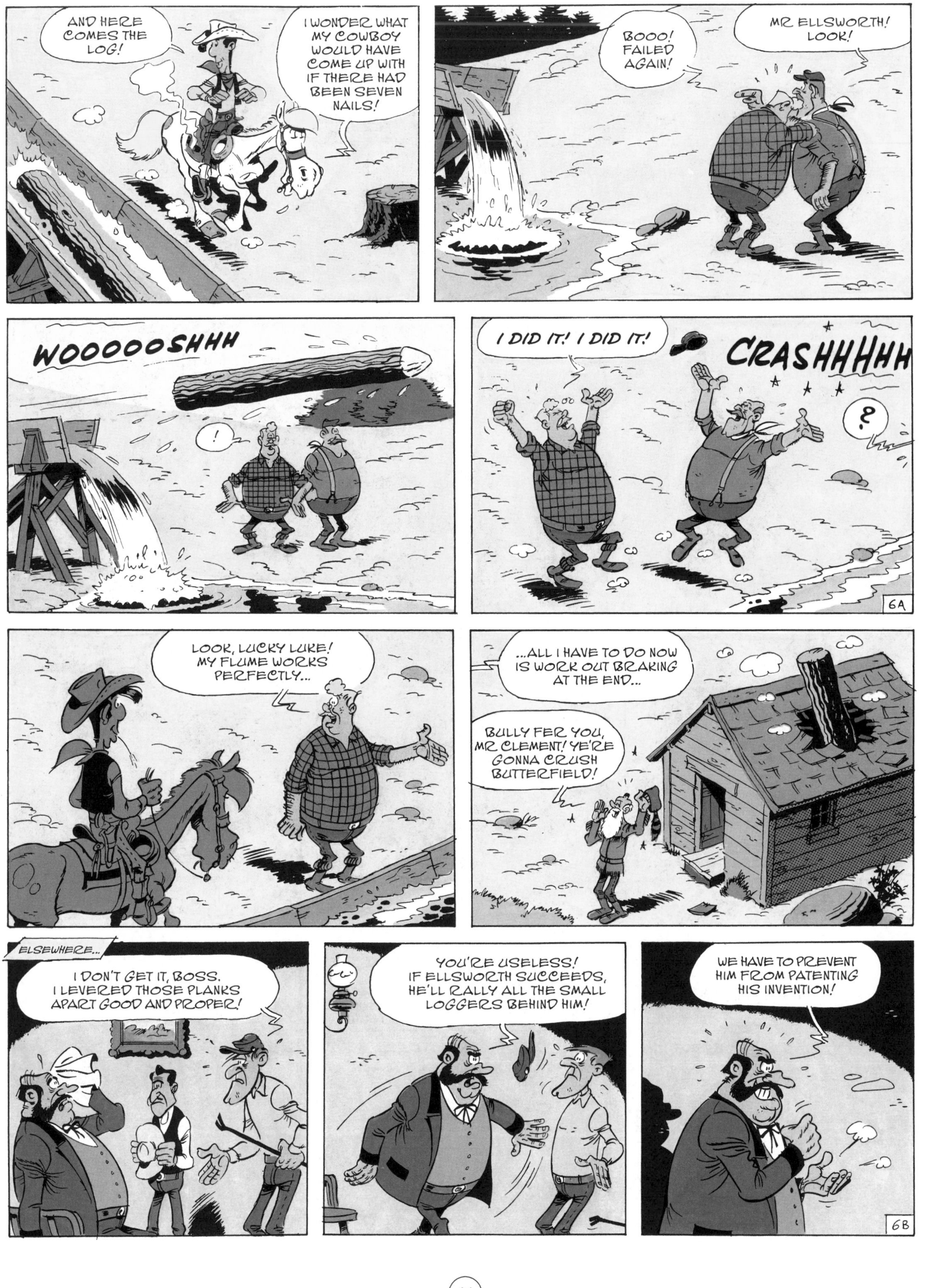
AND HERE COMES THE LOG!
I WONDER WHAT MY COWBOY WOULD HAVE COME UP WITH IF THERE HAD BEEN SEVEN NAILS!
BOOO! FAILED AGAIN!
MR ELLSWORTH! LOOK!
WOOOOOSHHH
!
I DID IT! I DID IT!
CRASHHHHH
?
6A
LOOK, LUCKY LUKE! MY FLUME WORKS PERFECTLY...
...ALL I HAVE TO DO NOW IS WORK OUT BRAKING AT THE END...
BULLY FER YOU, MR CLEMENT! YE'RE GONNA CRUSH BUTTERFIELD!
ELSEWHERE...
I DON'T GET IT, BOSS. I LEVERED THOSE PLANKS APART GOOD AND PROPER!
YOU'RE USELESS! IF ELLSWORTH SUCCEEDS, HE'LL RALLY ALL THE SMALL LOGGERS BEHIND HIM!
WE HAVE TO PREVENT HIM FROM PATENTING HIS INVENTION!
6B

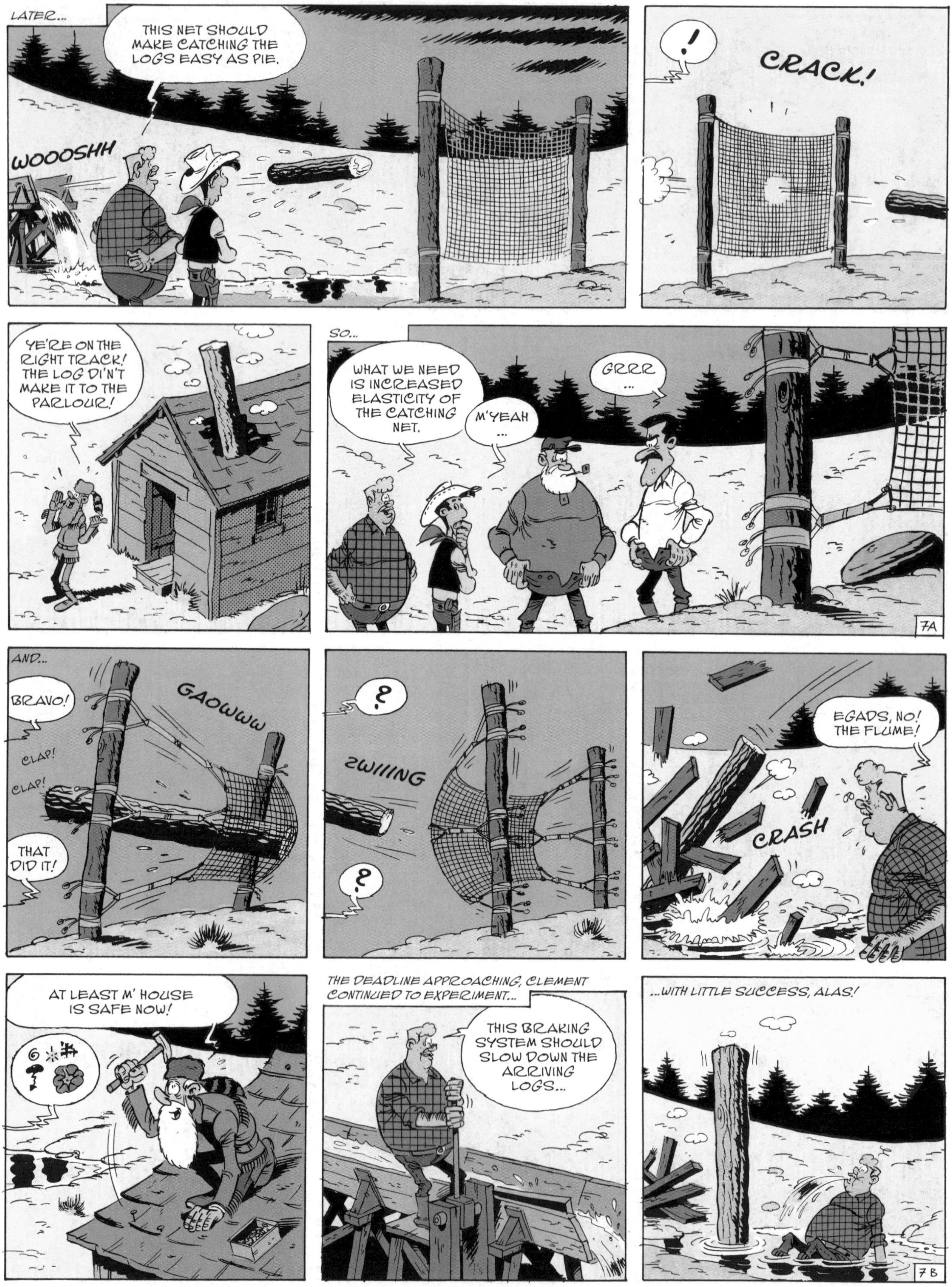

LATER...
THIS NET SHOULD MAKE CATCHING THE LOGS EASY AS PIE.
WOOOSHH
!
CRACK!
YE'RE ON THE RIGHT TRACK! THE LOG DI'N'T MAKE IT TO THE PARLOUR!
SO...
WHAT WE NEED IS INCREASED ELASTICITY OF THE CATCHING NET.
M'YEAH ...
GRRR ...
7A
AND...
BRAVO!
CLAP!
CLAP!
THAT DID IT!
GAOWWW
?
ZWIIING
?
EGADS, NO! THE FLUME!
CRASH
AT LEAST M' HOUSE IS SAFE NOW!
THE DEADLINE APPROACHING, CLEMENT CONTINUED TO EXPERIMENT...
THIS BRAKING SYSTEM SHOULD SLOW DOWN THE ARRIVING LOGS...
...WITH LITTLE SUCCESS, ALAS!
7B

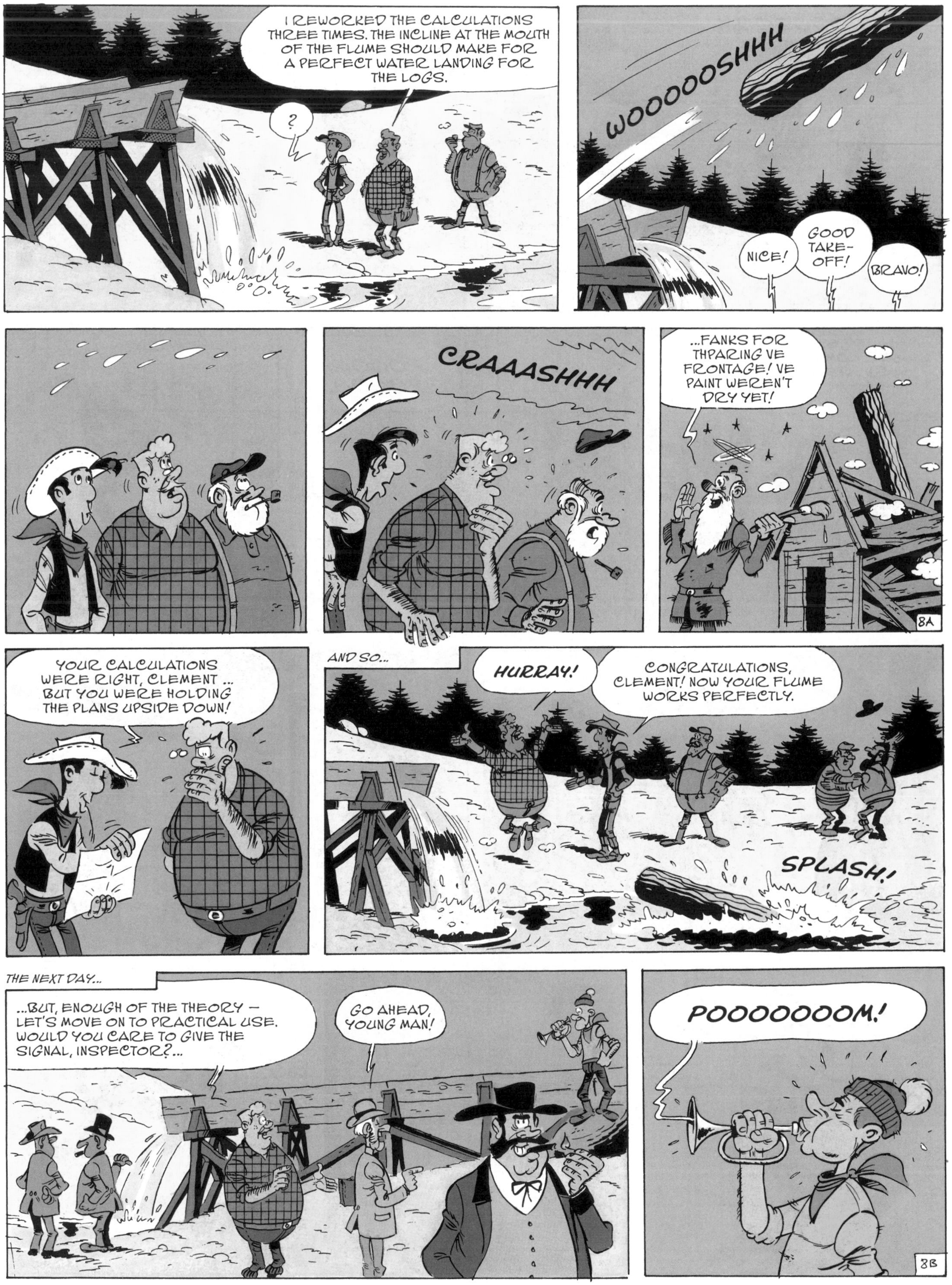

I REWORKED THE CALCULATIONS THREE TIMES. THE INCLINE AT THE MOUTH OF THE FLUME SHOULD MAKE FOR A PERFECT WATER LANDING FOR THE LOGS.
?
WOOOOOSHHH
NICE!
GOOD TAKE-OFF!
BRAVO!
CRAAASHHH
...FANKS FOR THPARING VE FRONTAGE! VE PAINT WEREN'T DRY YET!
8A
YOUR CALCULATIONS WERE RIGHT, CLEMENT ... BUT YOU WERE HOLDING THE PLANS UPSIDE DOWN!
AND SO...
HURRAY!
CONGRATULATIONS, CLEMENT! NOW YOUR FLUME WORKS PERFECTLY.
SPLASH!
THE NEXT DAY...
...BUT, ENOUGH OF THE THEORY – LET'S MOVE ON TO PRACTICAL USE. WOULD YOU CARE TO GIVE THE SIGNAL, INSPECTOR?...
GO AHEAD, YOUNG MAN!
POOOOOOOM!
8B

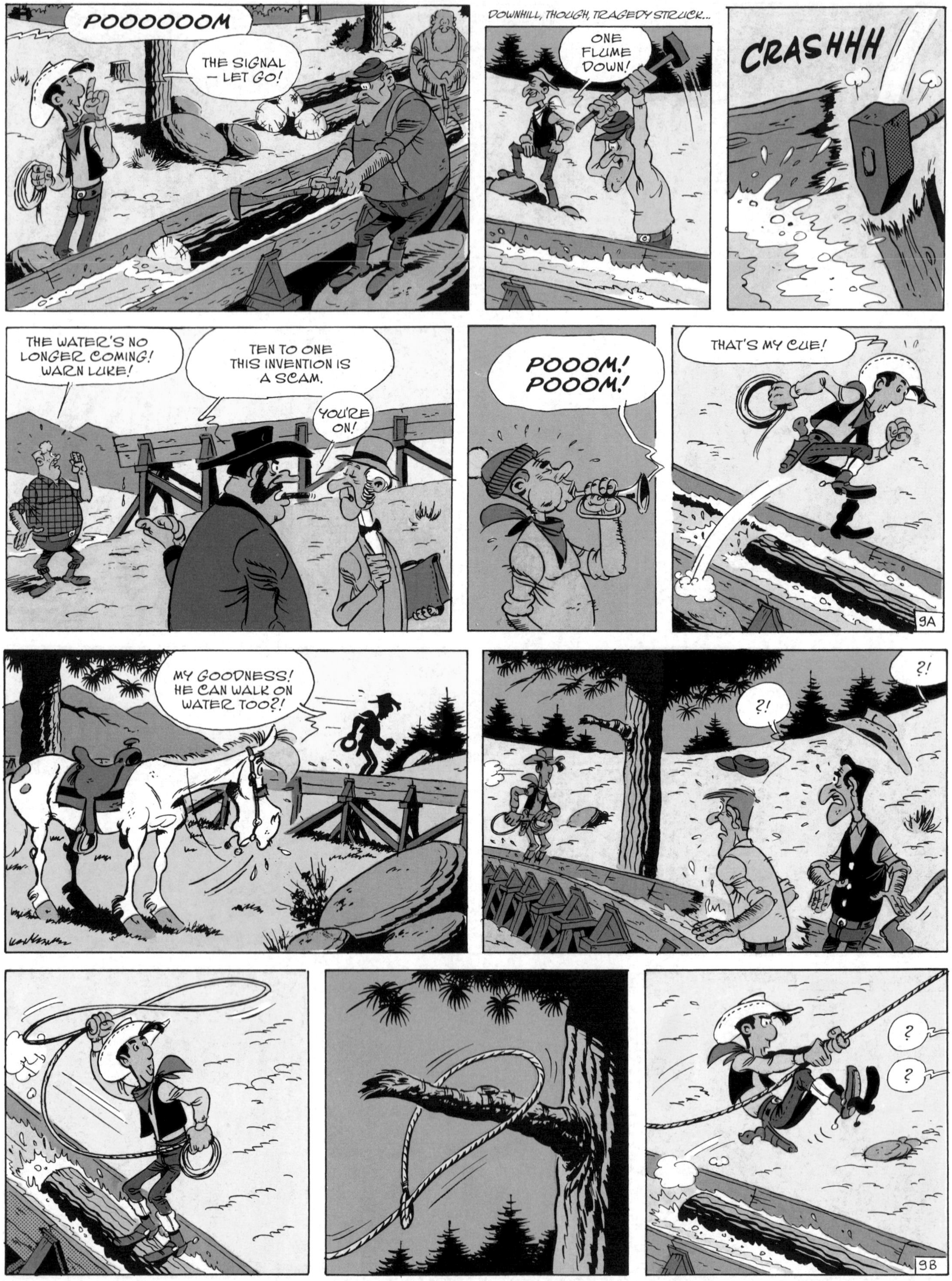

POOOOOOM
THE SIGNAL – LET GO!
DOWNHILL, THOUGH, TRAGEDY STRUCK...
ONE FLUME DOWN!
CRASHHH
THE WATER'S NO LONGER COMING! WARN LUKE!
TEN TO ONE THIS INVENTION IS A SCAM.
YOU'RE ON!
POOOM! POOOM!
THAT'S MY CUE!
9A
MY GOODNESS! HE CAN WALK ON WATER TOO?!
?!
?!
?
?
9B

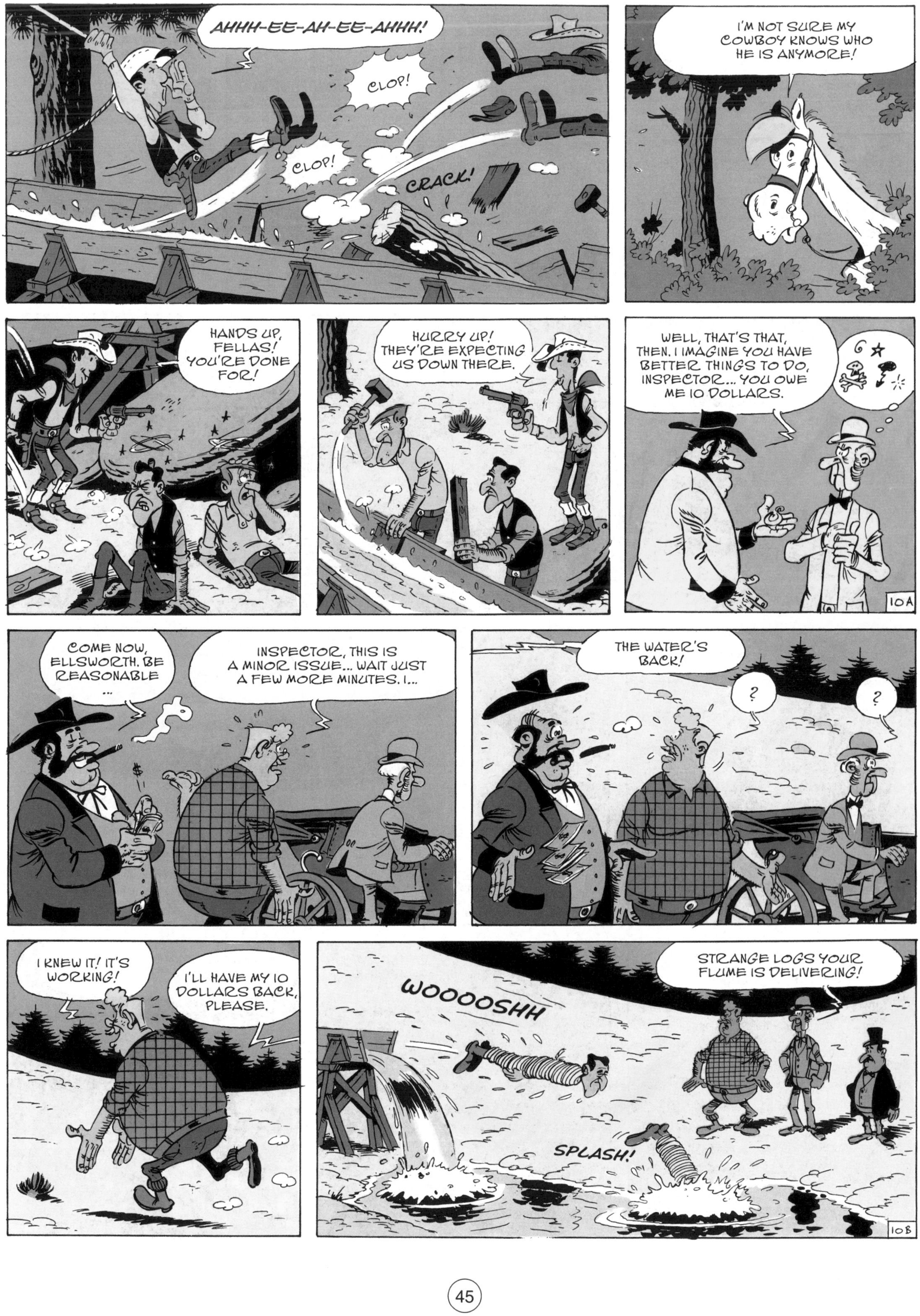
AHHH-EE-AH-EE-AHHH!
CLOP!
CLOP!
CRACK!
I'M NOT SURE MY COWBOY KNOWS WHO HE IS ANYMORE!
HANDS UP, FELLAS! YOU'RE DONE FOR!
HURRY UP! THEY'RE EXPECTING US DOWN THERE.
WELL, THAT'S THAT, THEN. I IMAGINE YOU HAVE BETTER THINGS TO DO, INSPECTOR... YOU OWE ME 10 DOLLARS.
10A
COME NOW, ELLSWORTH. BE REASONABLE ...
INSPECTOR, THIS IS A MINOR ISSUE... WAIT JUST A FEW MORE MINUTES. I...
THE WATER'S BACK!
?
?
I KNEW IT! IT'S WORKING!
I'LL HAVE MY 10 DOLLARS BACK, PLEASE.
WOOOOSHH
STRANGE LOGS YOUR FLUME IS DELIVERING!
SPLASH!
10B

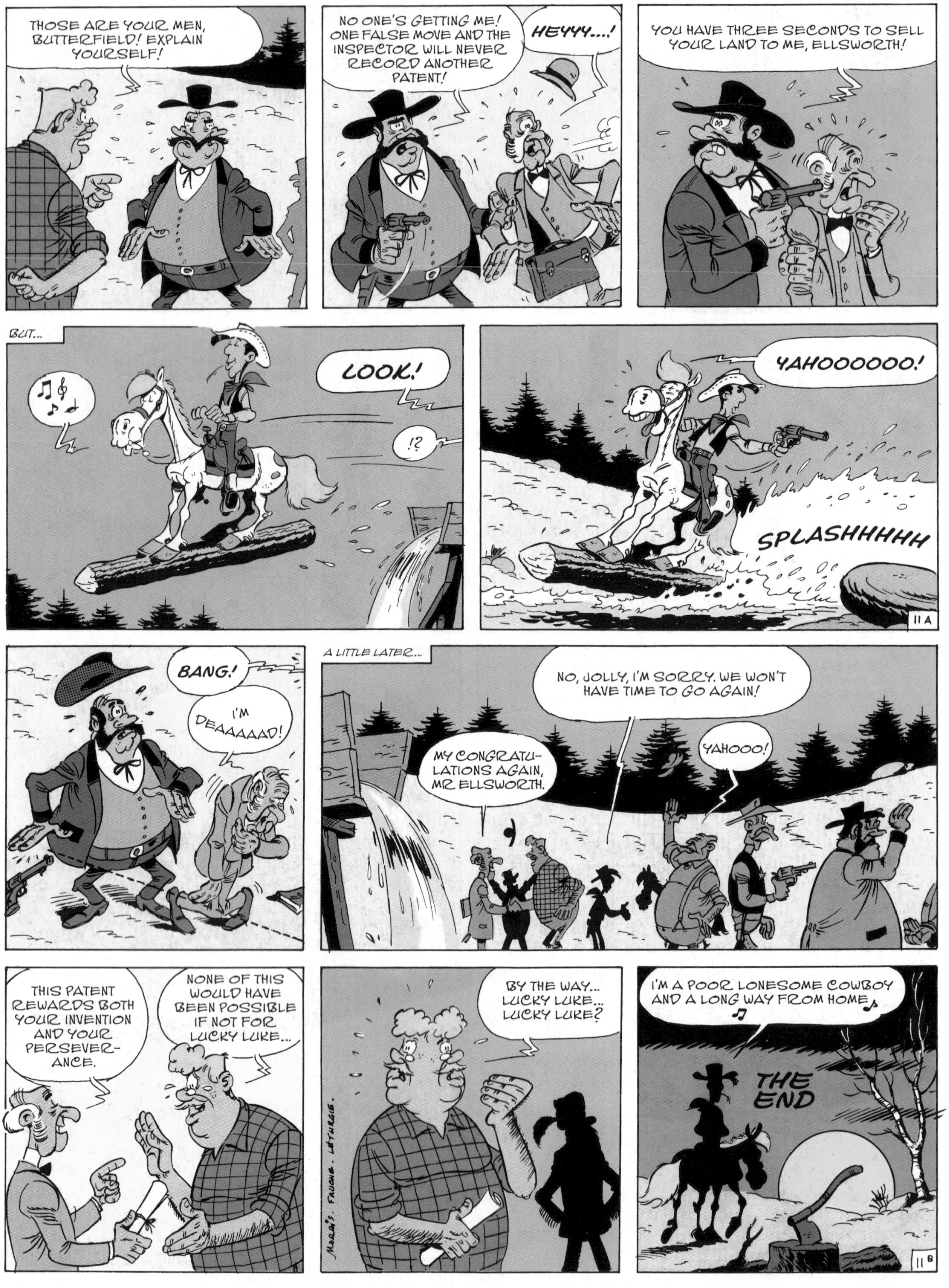
THOSE ARE YOUR MEN, BUTTERFIELD! EXPLAIN YOURSELF!
NO ONE'S GETTING ME! ONE FALSE MOVE AND THE INSPECTOR WILL NEVER RECORD ANOTHER PATENT!
HEYYY....!
YOU HAVE THREE SECONDS TO SELL YOUR LAND TO ME, ELLSWORTH!
BUT...
LOOK!
!?
YAHOOOOOOO!
SPLASHHHHH
11 A
BANG!
I'M DEAAAAAAD!
A LITTLE LATER...
NO, JOLLY, I'M SORRY. WE WON'T HAVE TIME TO GO AGAIN!
MY CONGRATULATIONS AGAIN, MR ELLSWORTH.
YAHOOO!
THIS PATENT REWARDS BOTH YOUR INVENTION AND YOUR PERSEVERANCE.
NONE OF THIS WOULD HAVE BEEN POSSIBLE IF NOT FOR LUCKY LUKE...
BY THE WAY... LUCKY LUKE... LUCKY LUKE?
I'M A POOR LONESOME COWBOY AND A LONG WAY FROM HOME
THE END
11 B